Thea Stilton
AND THE TREASURE SEEKERS

COMPASS OF
THE STARS

Scholastic Inc.

Library of Congress Cataloging-in-Publication Data available

ISBN 978-1-338-58740-1

Text by Thea Stilton
Original title *Tesori Perduti: La bussola di stelle*
Art Director: Iacopo Bruno
Graphic Designer: Francesca Leoneschi/theWorldof007
Cover by Alessandro Muscillo and Christian Aliprandi
Illustrations by Giuseppe Facciotto, Chiara Balleello, Barbara Pellizzari, Valeria Brambilla, and Alessandro Muscillo
Graphics by Laura Zuccotti

Special thanks to AnnMarie Anderson
Translated by Andrea Schaffer
Interior design by Becky James

10 9 8 7 6 5 4 3 2 1   20 21 22 23 24

Printed in China   62

First edition, April 2020

Dear friends,

We've just returned from an adventure we will never forget! Almost a century ago, a young archaeologist named Aurora Beatrix Lane discovered seven ancient treasures. Suddenly, we found ourselves involved in an extraordinary hunt for a precious new treasure. We traveled across an entire continent, over snowy landscapes covered in ice and through dry, dusty deserts scorched by a blazing sun. Along the way, we met fascinating new friends and solved a mystery. You can find out about the rest of our adventure by reading these pages. We hope the trip will excite you as much as it did us!

Big hugs from the Thea Sisters,

PAULINA

nicky

Violet   Colette

PAMELA

MEET THE THEA SISTERS!

Colette

She has a real passion for clothing and accessories, especially pink ones. When she is older she wants to be a fashion writer.

Paulina

She is generous and cheerful, and she loves traveling and meeting new people all over the world. She has a real knack for science and technology.

Violet

She loves reading and learning about new things. She likes classical music and dreams of becoming a famouse violinist!

Nicky

She comes from Australia and is passionate about sports, ecology, and nature. She loves the open air and is always on the move!

Pamela

She is a skilled mechanic: Give her a screwdriver and she can fix anything! She loves to cook. Her favorite food is pizza, and she would eat it every moment of every day if she could.

Do you want to be a Thea Sister?

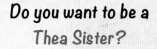

I like . . . _____
_____
_____
_____
_____

TRAPPED!

A small flame flickered in the **DARKNESS**, lighting up the room.

"Where are we?" Pam asked. She held a match* in her paw and moved it around slowly, trying to LIGHT UP the area around her.

"I think we're locked in the basement," Violet replied. "Pam, where did you find those matches?"

"At the restaurant we ate in last night," Pam replied. "It seems like every restaurant here in Russia has a bowl of matchbooks near the exit. I have at least five in my pocket!"

* Matches are dangerous. Never light a match without an adult's help.

She passed one to each of her friends.

"How clever of you to save them," Colette said gratefully.

"Let's be sure not to **BURN** our fur!" Nicky replied.

"Of course," Colette said reassuringly. "We'll be careful."

"Excuse me," squeaked a soft voice. "Can

I know where we are . . .

I have a match, too?"

"Of course, **Sergei**," Pam replied, and she passed him one.

"We need to find a way out of here quickly," Paulina said. She held her light up to the walls and began to push cautiously on them with her free paw.

"I know this **place**," Sergei said suddenly.

We need to find an exit!

"I came here a few times when I was doing a summer internship at the laboratory. This is where the scientists keep old documents and instruments they don't use anymore."

"We're in the **STORAGE ROOM** in the basement of the laboratory, then," Violet confirmed.

"Yes," Sergei said. "The door is always locked, and you need to punch a code into the digital keypad to get in and out."

"Do you know the code?" Nicky asked.

"No, I'm afraid not," Sergei replied. "I only know the code to enter the lab. This one must be different."

"Maybe someone will find us," Pam said, sighing.

But Violet shook her head. "Today is Saturday," she said. "The lab will be deserted until Monday. We can't stay locked down here for two days while Irina is in DANGER!"

We can't wait that long!

"Yes, and I could really use some fresh air," Nicky squeaked anxiously.

"She doesn't like small spaces," Violet explained quietly to Sergei.

"Nicky, just focus on breathing in and breathing OUT," Colette coached her friend gently. "If we all stay calm, we'll be fine."

"Good advice, Coco," Violet said encouragingly. But even as she spoke, Violet began to wonder: How had their vacation in Moscow taken such a DARK turn?

WELCOME TO MOSCOW

Everything started two days earlier, when the Thea Sisters landed at the Moscow airport.

"It's not as **cold** as I expected it to be," Violet admitted as she stepped off the plane.

"It would be even warmer if you had let me take you all to **Peru**!" Paulina teased her friend.

Peru!

Paris!

"Paris is also **lovely** in the spring..." Colette said, sighing.

China!

"CHINA would have been warmer, too," Violet agreed.

"Come on, sisters!" Nicky reminded them. "We chose Moscow so we could see **NEW** things and meet **NEW** mice."

"Nicky's right," Pam agreed. "Moscow is the perfect place to spend spring break!"

"**TAXI!**" Nicky called as she waved her paw at a car that was big enough to *transport* all five mice and their bags to their hotel.

After they loaded their suitcases into the trunk, the taxi headed toward the **center** of the city.

"Where's our hotel again?" Colette asked

Paulina, who was holding a guide to Moscow in one paw and a paper printed with every detail of their itinerary in the other.

"We're staying near the celebrated Red Square," Paulina replied. "That's where we'll find some of the most spectacular monuments in the city."

"We'll be just a short WALK from the beautiful Saint Basil's Cathedral!" Violet said enthusiastically.

"That sounds great, but I have one very **important** question," Pam replied.

"Do you want to know which museum we're planning to go to first?" Paulina asked.

Pam shook her head. "No, but does anyone

know if **breakfast** is included in our reservation?" she replied.

The other mice burst out in laughter as the taxi inched slowly through the heavy city traffic. After about an hour, the group finally reached their hotel.

Violet yawned and rubbed her eyes.

"I can't wait to take a little nap," she said **sleepily**.

"A nap?!" Nicky exclaimed. "But we don't have time for a nap! According to the itinerary that Paulina and I made, we're headed to Red Square right away."

"Yes, and tomorrow we head to a few museums and to the KREMLIN," Paulina continued.

"We absolutely must make time for a little

shopping," Colette said. "I know I'll find some beautiful items here in Moscow that I could never get on Whale Island!"

"Okay," Nicky agreed as she pulled a piece of paper from her pocket. "We'll make a **small** change to the itinerary."

"An eight-mile *RUN* in the park?!" Violet exclaimed after taking a peek at Nicky's itinerary. "Isn't this supposed to be a RELAXING break to recharge after our exams?"

"All right, all right," Nicky agreed good-naturedly. "We can make a few **BIG** changes to the schedule!"

"It's our turn!" Colette interjected. She gestured toward the reception desk, where a friendly mouse was waiting to help them check in.

"WELCOME!" greeted the receptionist warmly. Then she gave them the keys to their rooms and a **MAP** of the city. "We reserved two rooms for your group. The first sleeps two, and the other sleeps three. There's an adjoining door between the rooms.

Have a wonderful stay in Moscow!"

Welcome!

An Unexpected Mystery

The first two days the Thea Sisters spent in Moscow passed by in a **FLASH** as the mice dashed from lavish palaces to fascinating museums to a performance at a historic theater.

"I can't wait to try the **restaurant** the hotel recommended!" Pam squeaked eagerly as she and her friends walked along a bustling street in the city center. "I'm looking forward to **tasting** some authentic borscht."

"An authentic what?" Paulina asked, confused.

"It's a **beet soup** served with sour cream," Pam explained. Yum!"

"And I imagine once you've tasted some borscht you'll be satisfied?" Violet teased her friend.

"You are mistaken, sister," Pam replied. "If there's one thing I've learned while traveling, it's that even when you think you've tasted everything, there is always a new delicacy to discover!"

Paulina burst out laughing. "According to my map, the restaurant is close, and your dreams will come true!" she said.

"Oh my! Look!" Colette exclaimed suddenly. She pointed at a mouse who had just passed them and was walking in front of their group.

"What is it, Coco?" Nicky asked playfully. "Are you hoping to find boots like those on our shopping trip tomorrow?"

"No, look at her hair," Colette explained

seriously. "That **BaRRette** she's wearing reminds me of something, but I'm not sure what."

The five mice stared at the stranger. Her long, dark hair was pinned back with a pretty gold barrette in the shape of a small **ladybu**g.

"You're right," Nicky said thoughtfully. "I think I've seen it somewhere before, too. But where?"

"*I KNOW!*" Pam declared triumphantly. "It looks familiar because Ruby Flashyfur has the same barrette and wears it all the time at Mouseford Academy!"

Collette **shook** her head. "Ruby has a collection of clips shaped like butterflies, not ladybugs!" she said.

"This one also looks like an antique," Violet added. "Maybe it's a family heirloom."

"But of course!" Nicky exclaimed. "I know exactly why it looks so familiar. Let's follow her! Hurry!"

The Thea Sisters trusted their friend, who had begun to scurry ahead to close the gap between their group and the stranger.

That way!

Colette hurried after Nicky, tapping her arm lightly.

"Can you tell us what you thought of?" she asked, curious.

"**THE DIARY!**" Nicky replied, keeping her eye on the stranger. "Don't you remember?"

"What diary?" Colette replied, perplexed.

"Of course!" Violet exclaimed. "**Aurora's diary!** Now I remember, too. There's a **P H O T O** in the diary that shows one of Aurora's sisters wearing an identical barrette! I think her sister's name was Hannah . . ."

"You're right!" Colette gasped, astounded at the discovery. She and her friends had spent many nights *reading* the pages of the antique diary and admiring the fascinating photos. In one image, the explorer Aurora Beatrix Lane posed with her six SISTERS, one of whom was wearing a barrette that was the shape of a ladybug.

"If she has the barrette, she could be connected to Aurora," Paulina concluded. "We can't LOSE SIGHT of her!"

"Something tells me that I won't be trying borscht tonight after all," Pam mumbled to herself as she hurried after her friends.

The barrette!

The mouse they were following turned left and stopped suddenly in front of a building with a **LARGE GLASS DOOR**. Colette approached to squeak with the stranger, but before she could open her mouth, the mouse tapped a **code** into a keypad and disappeared inside the building.

A SUDDEN
REALIZATION

"Too late!" Colette exclaimed, her paws on the glass door that had closed behind the stranger.

"This looks like some type of **scientific laboratory**," Violet observed, peeking inside.

"What a shame," Nicky said. "It would have been interesting to find out if that mouse has anything to do with *Aurora*."

"We're probably wrong," Pam said with a shrug. "What are the chances that

Too late . . .

we would bump into a member of the *Lane* family here in Moscow? It doesn't seem very **likely**."

"You're right," Violet agreed. "We let our **imaginations** run wild!"

"The good news is that we still have time

to get to the **restaurant**!" Pam added.

"No," Nicky said.

"Yes, we do," Pam insisted. "It's only eight right now."

"No, I mean it wasn't our imagination!" Nicky exclaimed. "Look over there!"

She pointed inside of the building, where three shadows moved in the dim light.

"That can't be!" Violet gasped. "Those henchmice work for **KLAWITZ**! What are they doing in Moscow?"

"It really does look like Cassidy, Stan, and Max, doesn't it?" Colette agreed, pointing at the figures through the window.

LUKE VON KLAWITZ

A greedy, unscrupulous dealer of ancient art and antiques. He is a descendant of archaeology professor Jan von Klawitz.

CASSIDY

Klawitz's right-paw mouse. She organizes and coordinates his missions.

STAN AND MAX

These two rats work for Klawitz.

The five mice couldn't believe it. What were those three doing here in Moscow?

"Sisters, our intuition was right," Violet said. "If those three are here, that mouse with the barrette definitely has something to do with Aurora."

"And she's in DANGER!" Nicky suddenly realized. "We have to help her!"

BUT WHO ARE YOU?

The street in front of the laboratory was deserted. There was no one to ask for HELP.

"I will go see if there is a side entrance somewhere," Nicky said. "You try to figure out if we can get through the front door somehow."

Nicky *DARTED* around to the back of the building while her friends tried to find a way to get in the main entrance.

"We need a code," Colette said as she studied the digital keypad. "Paulina, do you think you could figure out how to OPEN the door without the code?"

"Hmm . . . let me see," Paulina replied. The others held their **breath** while

Paulina examined the keypad carefully.

After a few minutes, though, she shook her head.

"There's nothing I can do," she concluded. "You need the right combination to open it!"

A moment later, Nicky returned.

"Unfortunately, I couldn't find any other way in," she explained. "Did you have any luck opening the front door?"

"No, it's impossible without the code," Paulina replied.

"We've got to try somehow!" Colette exclaimed, a worried look on her snout. "I can't SEE Cassidy, Stan, and Max anymore."

"Sisters, knowing what we do about Klawitz's henchmice,

It's the only entrance!

27

shouldn't we go to the **POLICE**?" Pam suggested.

Right at that moment, a mouse about their age appeared from around the corner. He went up to the door and was about to tap a sequence into the **KEYPAD**.

We have to get in!

"Excuse me," Colette interrupted him. "Can you help us? We need to get into the building. A mouse inside is in **DANGER**!"

The mouse looked at them in shock. "What do you mean?"

"There is no time to explain right now," Nicky said urgently. "Please open the door, and then we promise to tell you **everything**!"

"But who are you?" the mouse asked, a

confused look on his snout. "And why are you squeaking about danger? This is a center for SCIENTIFIC RESEARCH. As far as I know, it's one of the most peaceful places in Moscow!"

But why?

The Thea Sisters exchanged a glance. If Klawitz was involved, they knew the situation was serious. But could they trust this stranger? Was it best to tell him everything they knew?

As they tried to decide what to do, they were interrupted by a frightened SCREAM from inside the laboratory.

"Oh no!" the stranger gasped, growing

pale. "That sounded just like my **Sister**, **Irina**!"

He quickly typed a **code** into the keypad and the door slid open. Without wasting another second, he hurried inside, with the Thea Sisters close behind.

THE GAME ENDS HERE

There were cries coming from the second floor of the laboratory.

"**Hold on, Irina!**" the boy called out. "I'm coming!"

Then he took off toward the stairs.

"Let's go with him!" Nicky said to her friends.

On the second floor, the Thea Sisters' **suspicion** was confirmed: Cassidy was restraining the mouse with the ladybug barrette by holding her paws behind her back. Max and Stan were there as well.

"Who are you?" the boy yelled. "And what are you doing to my sister?!"

"That's none of your business," Cassidy

replied. "In fact, I would advise you to disappear as soon as possible."

Then she noticed the five mice who had raced up the stairs with him.

"Wh-what are you **five** doing here?!" she gasped in DISBELIEF.

"We recognized you," Violet replied.

"And we'll figure out what you're up to again!" Paulina said, boldly crossing her paws across her chest.

Cassidy regained her composure quickly.

"Max, Stan," she called, "take care of these intruders immediately. I'll deal with the scientist, Irina."

Huh?!

Everything happened too quickly for the Thea Sisters to react. Stan and Max used their **STRENGTH** to restrain the group.

Cassidy continued to hold the scientist's paws behind her back so she couldn't escape.

"Well, well, well." She smirked. "The Thea Sisters have meddled in our affairs yet again. The game ends here, you nosy mice! Stan, Max: Lock these six where they can't bother us."

"With great pleasure," Stan replied. "I have a spot in mind that will do the trick!"

"**Irina!**" the boy yelled, trying uselessly to free himself from Stan's grip.

"Sergei!" the scientist replied. "Don't worry, we'll see each other soon!"

"I wouldn't count on that too much, my dear," Cassidy threatened.

In the meantime, the two **henchmice** led the Thea Sisters and Sergei down two flights of stairs to the basement. There was a large METAL door through which they could see what looked like a **DARK**, bare storage room.

"Here you go!" Stan said as he pushed the six mice into the room.

Stop!

Sergei!

"Make yourselves cozy," Max added with a sneer.

The metal door closed with a loud **click**, and the Thea Sisters suddenly found themselves in the **DARK**.

TiME FOR EXPLANATiONS

Thanks to Pam's collection of matchbooks, the Thea Sisters and Sergei were able to make a little light in the basement.

After a few minutes spent pushing on the walls, Paulina finally found the door.

"Look!" she cried out. "**It's right here!**"

Sergei hurried over and lit up the keypad next to the door. "You enter the code here to unlock it," he explained. "It's too bad we don't know **WHat** it is!"

"It seems Klawitz and his henchmice have gotten the best of us this time," Violet said, sighing.

"But what do you think they're looking for?" Pam asked.

"Some sort of treasure, I guess," Paulina replied. "Maybe Klawitz suspects Irina has one of the clues Aurora and Hannah Lane left behind."

"Hannah Lane . . . but that's my great-grandmother!" exclaimed Sergei.

The Thea Sisters exchanged a GLANCE. It seemed the moment had arrived to tell their new friend what they knew.

"It's a long story," Colette began. "For us, it began in Scotland. We were there on what should have been a relaxing vacation."

"But it quickly turned into a surprising adventure," Nicky explained.

Then she and the Thea Sisters told Sergei how they had met a distant descendent of Aurora Beatrix Lane, an archaeologist and explorer who lived many years ago.

She was born in England and was the

fourth of seven **sisters**. From very early in her life, she had an adventurous spirit that led her to learn how to ride motorcycles and fly planes.

She grew up to become an archaeologist who was passionate about **traveling** the world and looking for the most precious artifacts in history.

"Thanks to two of Aurora's **diaries** that we were lucky enough to find, we feel as if we really knew her," Violet explained, smiling.

"I've heard many stories about my great-grandmother's sister," Sergei explained. "At family dinners, there's always someone who brings up her name or one of her **LEGENDARY** adventures.

"To tell you the truth, I never fully believed those stories. I was almost convinced that she was a mythical figure rather than someone real!"

"It's really true," Pam confirmed. "Aurora

Beatrix Lane was a truly **extraordinary** mouse!"

Sergei still looked puzzled.

"What in the name of cheese does Irina have to do with any of this?" he said.

"We'll get there," Violet assured him. "Now, though, we should tell you the story about an incredible discovery that changed Aurora's life forever."

"Aurora discovered the legend of the seven treasures," Colette began.

"The seven treasures?" Sergei echoed.

Violet nodded. "There are seven treasures in the world, each one tied to some of the greatest figures in history. For a long time, many believed the treasures were a legend. But Aurora found clues that proved they exist. She made finding them her life's mission."

"She wanted to donate the treasures to museums and institutions around the world so that everyone could *admire* and learn from them," Nicky continued.

"But someone else was searching for them, too," Pam said. "Aurora's former professor, Jan von Klawitz, wanted them for his own **personal collection**!"

"Aurora was forced to race Klawitz from one treasure to the next," Nicky continued. "Her goal was to find all the treasures and hide them so her professor would never get his greedy paws on a single thing!"

"I see," Sergei said thoughtfully. "She planned to return for each treasure once the professor was off her trail, right?"

"Yes, but unfortunately that isn't what happened," Violet said sadly.

"Aurora and Professor von Klawitz both

disappeared in a mysterious airplane accident."

"Aurora was never able to finish her mission," Nicky added. "But she didn't want the treasures to be lost forever! So she left her sisters clues to each treasure's location."

"This is where your great-grandmother

Hannah comes into the story," Colette said. "Aurora probably gave her a clue to find one of the seven treasures!"

"Okay, but what does all of this have to do with my sister, **Irina**?" Sergei asked.

AN UNEXPECTED QUIZ

Nicky lit a new match and began to squeak.

"The three mice who captured your sister work for Luke von Klawitz, the great-grandson of Aurora's professor!"

She explained that Luke wanted to find all seven treasures. He planned to keep them in his own **private** collection, just as his great-grandfather would have done.

"We've already stopped him once," Violet added. "While in Scotland, we learned about a treasure called the **ALABASTER GARDEN**. As we searched the world for the mysterious garden, Cassidy, Stan, and Max tried to stop us every step of the way!"

"And now they're back in action," Colette

continued. It seems like Klawitz figured out that Aurora left clues to another treasure."

"They think Irina has **information** about the treasure's location?" Sergei asked. "But that's impossible!"

"I think anything's possible," Nicky replied seriously. "We must get out of here as soon as possible so we can help Irina!"

"Paulina, do you think you can use your **computer** skills to figure out how to unlock this door?" Colette asked.

"Let me lend you a paw," Sergei said. "I'm pretty good with computers, too. Maybe we can work together to **CRACK THE CODE**!"

Paulina and Sergei stared at the keypad.

"It's a six-digit number," Paulina observed.

"Six digits," Sergei mused. "Let's try the zip code!"

Sergei **tapped** the combination on the

keypad, but there was a loud buzz as some words appeared on a small screen.

"The code is *invalid*," he said, sighing. "But it looks like there are three security questions to unlock the door."

"It's worth a try," Nicky said. "We don't have any other options."

"Do you know the answer to the first one?" Pamela asked Sergei.

1. IN WHAT YEAR WAS THE LABORATORY FOUNDED?

2. WHEN WAS PENICILLIN DISCOVERED?

3. WHEN WAS THE FIRST COMPUTER INVENTED?

"My sister talks about the **laboratory** all the time," Sergei admitted. "I'm pretty sure it's 1982," he said finally.

Pam was about to enter the number, but Paulina stopped her.

"**WAIT!**" she said. "If the code is a six-digit number, I think we should enter just the last two digits for each answer."

"Are you sure?" Nicky asked, worried about getting it wrong.

Alexander Fleming

"Let's give it a try," Violet said. "Alexander Fleming discovered **PENICILLIN** in 1928. If Paulina is right, then the first numbers are 82 and 28. But I can't answer the last question."

"I think it's 1946,"

Sergei said. "That's the year the ENIAC, the ELECTRONIC NUMERICAL INTEGRATOR AND COMPUTER went public."

"But in 1941, German Konrad Zuse invented the Z3, the first computer,"

Konrad Zuse

Paulina interjected. "It was destroyed in 1945, but it's possible that's the correct date for when the first computer was invented, not 1946."

Sergei thought it over for a MINUTE. Finally, he nodded.

"I agree," he said. "Let's go with 822841."

The Thea Sisters held their breath as Sergei punched the code into the keypad. A second later, the door clicked opened and the six friends hurried outside.

MORE QUESTIONS THAN ANSWERS

"Let me go!" Irina shouted. "I didn't do anything!"

"If you cooperate and answer a few questions," Cassidy said calmly, "you'll get to go home soon."

Then she turned on a large touch-screen MONITOR in front of the chair. Cassidy tapped a few commands directly on the screen, and a BLUE SCREEN lit up in front of them.

"We're connected," Cassidy announced. "Can we begin?"

"Move over, Cassidy," barked a dry, hard voice coming from the monitor. "I can't see our guest."

Cassidy stepped aside.

"Good afternoon, Dr. Irina Lenenko," the mouse on the screen greeted Irina. "I'm very happy to meet you."

Irina stared at the **BLUE SCREEN**. She had never seen this mouse before.

"Who are you?" she asked. "And what do you want from me?"

"All I want is a little information," he replied briskly.

"But there must be a mistake!" Irina protested. "I'm just a researcher. I don't have any valuable scientific info to share!"

"Oh, I'm not interested in science," he replied. "I'm interested in family **SECRETS**."

"What are you talking about?" Irina asked, a puzzled look on her snout.

"The better question is *who* am I talking about," he replied. "Does the name Hannah Lane mean anything to you?"

"Yes, she was my great-grandmother," Irina replied in astonishment. Without thinking, she brought her paw up to touch the ladybug barrette she wore in her hair. How did this mouse know her great-grandmother?

But . . . what?

"That's a lovely jewel you inherited from her," the mouse on the screen said.

"She . . . how did you know?" Irina asked aghast.

"I know many things," the mouse growled. "But I'm missing some key details. As soon as you help me, you'll be free to go.

"I understand that *Aurora Beatrix Lane* trusted her sister Hannah with a very precious secret," he continued. "It's something that was then carried down from mother to daughter — from Hannah to your grandmother, then to your mother, and then down to you."

"I don't have any idea what you're talking about," Irina replied.

The mouse sighed.

"If you refuse to cooperate, Cassidy can make this much harder for you."

"You have no right to

threaten me!" Irina squeaked indignantly.

"Enough!" the mouse shouted. "What do you know about the queen's jewel?"

"I . . . I don't know anything!" Irina replied.

"And what do you know about your great-grandmother Hannah?" he asked.

Irina remained silent.

"It will be much better for you if you tell us everything right away," Cassidy said menacingly. "Don't you want to see your brother again soon?"

Irina took a deep breath. "All I know is that my great-grandmother left England as a girl because she fell in love with a young Russian mouse. They lived together in Saint Petersburg."

"Yes, we already knew that," the mouse said. "Go on, continue."

SAINT PETERSBURG

LONDON

"I . . . I don't remember anything else," Irina said softly.

"Dr. Lenenko, I'm sorry you're so reluctant to speak with me," the mouse on the screen said menacingly. "Cassidy, get to work."

Luke von Klawitz **pressed** a button and the video call ended, Irina Lenenko's snout disappearing from his screen. He was sitting in his **SECRET** laboratory in Alaska, brooding over the unhelpful scientist. If only she had told him something **NEW**!

Klawitz opened the notebook sitting on the desk in front of him. The writing on the first page read:

Aurora Beatrix Lane
Diary 3

"This time your puzzles won't protect your secret, Aurora," he growled. "I'll decipher your riddles one by one, and your treasure will soon be **MINE**!"

THE SECRETS IN THE TRUNK

Sergei and the Thea Sisters checked the **laboratory** from top to bottom, searching for Irina. But Irina, Cassidy, Stan, and Max were nowhere to be found!

"What do we do now?" Pam asked, discouraged.

"Let's keep looking," Nicky said. "They can't have **gone** very far."

"I have an idea!" Sergei said eagerly. "I have a computer program at home that lets me see the location of my **sister's** cell phone. Come on, I don't live far from here!"

"Great!" Pam cheered. "Let's hurry!"

Fifteen minutes later, the six friends entered the apartment Sergei shared with his sister. The space was small but very warm and welcoming. There were travel mementos and family photos all over the living room.

"Wait here and I'll get my laptop from my bedroom," Sergei said.

A moment later, he had returned with the computer in his paws.

Paulina sat next to him, and the pair studied the screen closely.

"Oh no!" Sergei exclaimed suddenly.

"What's wrong?" Pam asked, SURPRISED.

"The satellite detector connected to my

Oh no!

sister's phone says that she's still at the **laboratory**!"

"But how is that possible?" asked Colette. "We looked for them everywhere!"

"Maybe she dropped her phone," Pam said. "Or perhaps Cassidy and the others took it from her and **left** it in the lab on purpose."

"And we don't have any other way to trace her," Nicky said, sighing heavily.

"Sergei, do you have some family mementos that might be useful?" Violet asked. "Maybe something **Hannah** left to you, or something that might help us understand what Luke von Klawitz wants from Irina."

At first, Sergei **shook** his head.

"I don't think so," he said. "My mother kept everything. Unless . . . follow me!"

The group moved to Irina's room. The shelves and walls were covered with certificates and trophies from different universities and **SCIENCE COMPETITIONS**.

Sergei pointed at a large **TRUNK**.

"Here it is," he said. "My sister keeps family mementos in here."

A cloud of **dust** rose up around them as it opened.

"This will be a tough job," Violet said as she took in the large pile of papers, boxes, and **dusty** old photographs.

"We can do it!" Nicky said. "Let's get started."

After just a **few minutes**, Paulina had a breakthrough.

"Oh, look! I think I found something!" she said. In her paws she held a bundle of old letters.

"I recognize that *writing*!" Colette exclaimed, pointing at the envelopes. "It's Aurora's!"

Violet delicately extracted an envelope from the pile.

"Coco's right," she said. "These are letters *Aurora Beatrix Lane* wrote to her sister Hannah!"

"You really think these old letters could contain *clues* for our search?" Sergei asked doubtfully.

"Knowing Aurora, I'm sure!" Violet reassured him, smiling.

The friends sat in a circle around the trunk and began to *quickly* read the letters, looking for details or information that could help them in some way.

"Here!" exclaimed Colette enthusiastically, waving one of the *letters*.

May 28

Dear Hannah,

It's been a long time since I've been able to write to you. Of course, it isn't because you haven't been in my thoughts! Rather, it's because something unexpected entered my life. My last mission brought me very close to finding an extraordinary treasure. I hope that all is going well in Saint Petersburg and that you and Ivan are always as happy as the day you met. Sometimes I envy your serenity a bit. But destiny has something else in store for me. It seems like my adventures are only just beginning. I hope to see you soon. Until then, I'm sending you a big hug.

Your affectionate sister,

Aurora

"I knew it," Paulina reflected. "One of the legendary seven treasures is involved again."

"And Aurora's words will be our map to find it!" Violet concluded.

The letter mentions a treasure!

We will find it!

JOURNEY DEEP IN THE NIGHT

Everyone reflected on what to do **next**.

"Luke von Klawitz probably has the same information about Hannah that we do," Violet said.

"Do you think he knows that she lived in SAINT PETERSBURG?" Sergei asked.

Violet nodded. "Yes, I think so. But we do have an *advantage*," she pointed out. "These letters are like a trail we can follow to find your **sister**!"

"Well then, let's not waste any time," Sergei exclaimed. "Let's go straight to Saint Petersburg."

"That's a great idea, but it's **VERY LATE**," Paulina pointed out. "I think we need to wait until tomorrow morning to *LEAVE* Moscow."

But Sergei shook his head. "There is a **night train** that leaves Moscow at midnight and arrives in Saint Petersburg at eight in the morning."

"That's *perfect*!" Colette exclaimed happily. "That gives us just enough time to return to our hotel for our bags."

Sergei packed some clothing and his cell phone in a backpack. Soon he and the Thea Sisters were hurrying toward the subway. They would make **two stops**: first, the hotel, and then the train station.

When they saw the beauty of the Moscow subway stations, the Thea Sisters were *breathless*.

"How elegant!" Colette exclaimed when they arrived at Komsomolskaya station. "I don't think I've ever seen such a beautiful subway station!"

The five friends admired the large columns, the decorated ceilings, and the grand chandeliers.

"Let's hurry," Sergei urged them. "The train won't wait!"

The six friends scurried into the platform, where they bought TICKETS and got on the midnight train.

"We did it!" Pam exclaimed, throwing herself on the elegant velvet bunk in relief.

"As long as the bunk is comfortable, I'll be happy," Violet said, yawning sleepily.

Knock, knock!

"Who on earth could that be at this time

of night?" Sergei asked, incredulous.

A second later, Colette and Nicky peeked into their train compartment.

"Sorry," Nicky said apologetically. "We

know it's **LATE**, but we thought we could read a few more letters before bed."

"Sure!" Paulina replied as she pulled the letters out of her bag and cleared her throat.

Dear Hannah,

How are you? How is Ivan? I think of you
all the time together with your sweetheart
in beautiful Saint Petersburg. At least
you always liked the cold, my dear sister!
Though I have never traveled to Russia, you
know I hope to come see you soon. One of
my archaeologist colleagues is from there,
and she warned me about the winters. I hope
Mother helped pack your suitcase with a lot
of warm coats and wool sweaters . . .

I have been absorbed by my work, which
is keeping me busier than ever. Do you
remember the extraordinary treasure that
I mentioned in my last letter? Well, dear
Hannah, my discovery made me think of you
and your passion for precious jewelry. Have
you ever heard of the queen's jewel?

I have so many things to tell you about it,
but I prefer to do it the next time I see you in
the fur! I hope I can make the trip soon.

A kiss to you and a hug to your husband.

Yours,
Aurora

P.S. I attached a
recent photo, as
you requested.
It's one of the
rare times I
got dressed
up to attend a
ball with dear
Robert!

A GREAT QUEEN

The first rays of the morning sun filtered through the thick curtains of the train compartment early the next morning.

Aurora's letters were full of **mysterious** hints about her travels and unusual anecdotes and passages in which she revealed secrets of her work. The six friends had been so absorbed that they were reading for hours.

"Ah, what a stiff neck!" Nicky complained as she stretched. She and Colette had been too tired to **drag** themselves back to their own compartment. Instead, they wound up sharing the compartment with Paulina and Pam.

"Maybe we should have **slept** in our own bunk," Nicky moaned, rubbing her neck.

"Maybe," Colette agreed, stretching as best as she could in the tiny space she shared with Pam. "Someone woke me up a bunch of times by **POKING** me with her elbows."

"Well, you were **snoring** very loudly!" Pam replied.

"Me?!" Colette protested. "I don't snore at all!"

"Of course you do," Pam replied, chuckling.

"Let's just get dressed," Paulina interrupted. "We're approaching the Saint Petersburg station!"

The six friends got ready **quickly** and left the train just in time.

"What's our next move?" Nicky asked.

"Before we do anything else, we have to get something to eat," Pam replied decisively. "Let's go to a café for breakfast!"

"I know a place right near here," Sergei said. "It's on Nevsky Prospekt, the most *famouse* street in Saint Petersburg. What do you say?"

"That sounds wonderful!" Pam said enthusiastically.

A few moments later, they were all seated around a table in an *elegant* café.

"Ah, I needed this!" Colette commented as she sipped a cup of hot black tea.

"Let's focus. The letters that we read yesterday mentioned the queen's jewel more than once," Paulina said. "What could that be about?"

Violet furrowed her brow. "It could be a crown or a scepter," she said.

"We really don't know for sure, do we?" Colette asked, a worried look on her snout.

"No, not really," Violet replied. "But when you think of a famouse royal here in Saint Petersburg, the first one that comes to mind is . . ."

"Catherine II!" Sergei said. "She was the most famouse EMPRESS in Russian history."

"Exactly," Violet said, smiling.

"If you're right, we must visit historical places in Saint Petersburg that are related to Catherine II," Paulina said. "Maybe we will find clues about the jewel there!"

CATHERINE II
(CATHERINE THE GREAT)

Born Sophie Friederike Auguste, Prinzessin von Anhalt-Zerbst, she was the daughter of a German prince. She married the heir to the Russian throne. In 1762, she herself became empress. Catherine II was a political and social reformer. Her main interests were in education and culture.

A DEAD END

Sergei downloaded a detailed map of Saint Petersburg onto his computer. He and Paulina planned to search for buildings and monuments connected to Catherine II.

"The jewel must be hidden and well protected, maybe in an antique **SAFE**," Nicky mused.

"It could have been hidden by the empress herself," Colette added. "Maybe Aurora discovered the hiding place."

"But how do we find it?" Pam asked. "We don't have Aurora's archaeological experience to guide us."

"But we have her letters!" Violet said, waving one of them. "Listen to this . . ."

Dear Hannah,

How are you? Are you feeling better after that awful cold you mentioned in your last letter? And how is Ivan? My work here is busier than ever, and unfortunately there are some who try to hinder me at every turn. But I don't want to tire you with boring details. Just know that the mission tied to the queen's jewel proceeds in spite of everything. I'm very close to my goal. Oh, and I almost forgot the most important thing: I am planning a trip to Russia! I absolutely must see the wonderful palaces of Saint Petersburg and its surroundings. I am especially interested in seeing the famouse Catherine Palace, with its Amber Room. My dear sister, I look forward to seeing you. I hope we can spend time together again, like we did when we were young mouselets.

Yours,
Aurora

"This letter mentioned the jewel . . . and Catherine Palace!" Nicky exclaimed.

"Let's start there!" Sergei said.

The group hailed two taxis and headed to the Catherine Palace, located in Pushkin,

How gorgeous!

about fifteen miles from the center of Saint Petersburg.

"Wow!" Colette exclaimed. "What a beautiful place."

"Where should we look first?" Sergei wondered aloud.

"The letter mentioned the Amber Room, the most beautiful and famouse room in the palace," Paulina replied. "Let's start there."

The group entered the palace and walked through the rich halls.

"It's too bad we don't have time for a real visit," Violet whispered, a little sadly.

"We have a mission to complete," Nicky replied. "Hopefully the queen's jewel will bring us to Irina. It's the only lead we have."

Finally, the group arrived at the Amber Room. The six mice looked around, breathless.

"It feels like we're inside a magical TREASURE CHEST," Colette murmured as she admired the sparkling walls. Every inch of the room seemed to be covered in elegant panels decorated with precious amber.

"The queen's jewel could be hidden in plain sight in this room," Nicky noticed.

"Or maybe there's a secret passage somewhere," Violet suggested.

"The Amber Room was a gift from the king of Prussia to Peter the Great in 1716 to celebrate peace between Prussia and Russia," a tour guide standing behind Violet squeaked. "During World War II, Nazi forces looted the room, removing the amber panels and sending them to Germany, where they were eventually lost. The room you see here is a reconstruction that was completed in 2003."

"Did you hear that?" Pam asked, dismayed. The friends nodded.

"If that's true, then this room can't be *Aurora's* hiding place," Paulina said. "Her travels dated to before the war!"

The Thea Sisters LOOKED crestfallen. They had reached a dead end!

"Then we must search elsewhere," Sergei said. "But where? The palace is immense!"

"Let's divide into groups and search every corner of the palace," Nicky said in a determined voice.

They turned to leave, but suddenly Violet stopped.

"Wait!" she squeaked. "Look at those two mice!"

The friends turned and clearly saw **MAX** and **Stan** at the other end of the hallway!

BACK TO THE CITY

"They must be looking for the queen's jewel, just like we are!" Paulina exclaimed. "Let's try to figure out where they're going."

The group began to trail the pair as they moved from one room of the palace to another. They were careful to be very quiet and to stay far enough back that they wouldn't be noticed.

Max and Stan moved methodically from one room to the next, but they didn't seem to find anything of interest.

"We've been following them for a while now and I have to be HONEST: It doesn't seem like they have any idea where to find the jewel!" Colette whispered softly.

"Look, they're leaving!" Pam said as the pair headed for the exit.

"Let's follow them!" Sergei exclaimed. "It's the only trail that can lead us to Irina."

The six **FRIENDS** left the palace and watched as Stan and Max got into a *sports car* and sped away.

"Taxi!" Nicky exclaimed as she hailed a van large enough for six passengers. The six mice quickly scrambled inside.

"Follow that car," Pam said, pointing at the ORANGE sports car.

The ride back to Saint Petersburg was **tense**, as the taxi driver stayed close to the sports car. Suddenly, Stan and Max parked in front of a small GRAY building on the city outskirts.

Sergei was about to get out of the taxi, but Paulina grabbed his arm.

"Wait, we can't **RISK** them seeing us!" she said.

Max and Stan entered the building, the door closing behind them. A second later, Sergei and the Thea Sisters approached the building quietly. They looked around for another entrance, but the **GRAY** building seemed to have just one: the opaque **GLASS** door Stan and Max had used.

It's Irina's!

Suddenly, Sergei picked up something from the street.

"She's here!" he exclaimed, holding

the yellow scarf in his paws. "This is Irina's. She must have dropped it when they brought her here."

"That means Irina is probably inside this building," Violet said. "We need to

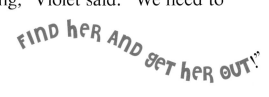

FIND heR AND geT heR OUT!"

RESCUE MISSION

The group quickly came up with a **PLAN**.

"Is everyone ready?" Violet asked.

"Yes, let's go!" everyone replied in unison.

Violet leaned cautiously around the corner of the building, checking the entrance.

"Okay, it's quiet out front," she reported. "Go!"

Pam and Nicky sprinted quickly toward the entrance, and Nicky **KNOCKED LOUDLY** three times.

Someone opened the door slightly. The dim light inside the building illuminated Stan's snout.

"B-but what," Stan stuttered in surprise. "You?!"

Pam and Nicky quickly put the next part of their plan into action: They turned and *RAN*.

"Max!" Stan shouted behind him. "It's those **nosy** mice again! I'm going after them!"

As the Thea Sisters had

Don't let them see us . . .

predicted, Stan and Max took the bait and headed out in pursuit of Nicky and Pam.

"Where do you think you're going?" Stan called as Pam and Nicky sprinted down an alley.

"**STOP!**" Max cried in frustration.

Meanwhile, Violet squeaked in delight.

"Our plan worked!" she exclaimed. "They ran after Pam and Nicky and left the door WIDE open!"

Violet, Sergei, Paulina, and Colette snuck inside the building.

"I'll stand **guard** here," Violet said as she stopped just inside the entrance.

Sergei, Colette, and Paulina tiptoed farther inside. The LIGHT that entered from the strip of windows under the roof allowed them to see a large, bare room with a small table and a few **rickety** chairs.

There were old wooden boxes scattered here and there. They didn't see Irina.

"Wait . . . don't you hear that SOUND?" Colette asked.

The three mice stood perfectly still as they strained their ears.

THUMP, THUMP.

The muffled sound was coming from a pile of WOODEN planks.

They moved the planks aside and followed the noise. They discovered a hidden closet. The door was locked from the outside.

Sergei hurried to open it, and his sister almost fell into his arms.

"Are you okay?" the boy asked, worried.

"Yes, I'm fine now that you **found me**!" she reassured him. "Those terrible mice locked me in here, but I'm okay."

"I'm sorry to interrupt, but we have to get out of here before those two return!" Paulina urged, a worried look on her snout.

At that moment, Violet squeaked from the entrance.

"They're coming! We need to GO!"

Sergei took Irina's paw and led her outside quickly, followed by Violet, Colette, and Paulina.

A few moments later, Max and Stan were back in the building.

Max went straight to the closet to check on the captive.

"She's gone!" he shouted, clenching his paws angrily.

"Let's keep that to ourselves," Stan said carefully. "I don't want problems with Cassidy and the boss. Am I wrong, or were there more than two of them when we were in **Moscow**?"

"Bah, what difference does it make?" Max grumbled. "They got the best of us this time."

A REVELATION

"What incredible teamwork!" Colette said, complimenting her friends.

"I don't think I've ever run so *FAST*," Nicky panted, still catching her breath. "If that had been a race, I'm sure I would have set a new record!"

"We need to go," Pam said, concerned. "Stan and Max are going to realize Irina escaped, and they'll be after us in no time."

"I have a friend who runs a **hotel** here in Saint Petersburg," Irina said. "If someone has a phone, I'll call him now."

An hour later, the group was settling into a large suite at the hotel.

To Pam's delight, they quickly ordered a

lavish dinner, which was delivered to their room.

"So you are friends of my brother?" Irina asked as she munched on a sandwich.

"In short, yes!" Paulina replied with a smile. She pulled out the letters they had found in Irina's trunk and began to tell Irina all they knew about *Aurora Beatrix Lane* and the mysterious queen's jewel.

"There was a mouse who asked me about the jewel over a video call," Irina explained.

"That must have been Luke von Klawitz," Colette replied. "He's related to Professor Jan von Klawitz, Aurora's former mentor."

"And did you tell him anything?" Violet asked.

Irina shook her head.

"I don't know anything about the queen's jewel," she replied. "And even if I did, I would never have told him. I didn't even tell him what I know about **Hannah** and *Aurora*. But I'll tell all of you . . ."

A solemn silence fell over the group. Irina opened her mouth to squeak, and Pam noisily ate a spoonful of her **SOUP**.

"Slurp!"

"Come on, Pam," Colette said, groaning. "Is this the best time for snacking?"

"Sorry," Pam replied, shrugging. "I've waited three days to try borscht, and I must say that it's **delicious**!"

Colette sighed and the others burst out **laughing**.

When everyone had quieted down, Irina began her story.

"My grandmother told me she received an unexpected visit from Aurora once, but not here in Saint Petersburg," she explained. "It happened after Hannah and her husband had transferred to **SIBERIA**, her husband's homeland, near the Ob River, in western Siberia. I can show you the exact spot on a map."

"Are you telling us that's where we're headed next?" Nicky asked.

Irina smiled.

"I have to go back to Moscow," she said. "But my brother will go with you!"

THE NEXT MOVE

Meanwhile, deep underground in **frigid** Alaska, Luke von Klawitz's secret base was full of activity.

The monitors in his laboratory transmitted images of every angle of the globe. But despite all the technology at his disposal, Klawitz was still lacking vital information.

"I can't believe those two let her get away," he muttered, clenching his paws and shaking his head. He had just hung up the phone and had learned about Irina's **escape**.

Now all of the research he'd done into **Hannah's** descendants had gone to waste. After a moment, though, Luke von Klawitz had decided on a **NEW PLAN**. He turned on

Hannah

Irina

the computer to his left and gave a voice command.

"Call Petrovski," he said, and the computer automatically began dialing a telephone **number**.

"Is that you, Klawitz?" came a **low voice** with a Russian accent a moment later.

"Good morning, Petrovski," he replied.

"It's been a long time," Petrovski said. "How is business?"

"Good," Klawitz replied. "I just have a **small** problem."

"Can I help you?" asked Petrovski. "As

you know, I am happy to assist you with contacts and information if I can."

"Do you still have access to the lists of all of the passengers leaving from and arriving at Russian **airports**?"

"Of course."

"Good. I need to track down six mice leaving Saint Petersburg."

It only took a few minutes for Klawitz's friend to give him a response: The Thea Sisters and **Sergei** were headed to Novosibirsk, in Siberia.

"Siberia," Klawitz said in a low voice. "I wonder what those nosy little mice are up to now."

He tapped a few keys on the control panel next to his monitor, which sat right near Aurora's diary.

Klawitz quickly rifled through the pages until he found a PICTURE of a smiling Aurora and her sister Hannah. The countryside was behind them.

He removed the photo and placed it on a scanner. Then he typed Novosibirsk, Siberia on the keyboard.

A moment later, the program was comparing the landscape from the photo with other images of **Novosibirsk**. After about thirty seconds, there was a match! The program provided Klawitz with the exact coordinates of the place where the photo had been taken.

He quickly called Cassidy.

"Good morning, sir," she answered through her wrist communicator. "I am searching the Lenenko house. I haven't found anything useful except an empty envelope with *Aurora Beatrix Lane's* address listed as the sender. The letter is missing, though."

Klawitz waved his paw in the air dismissively.

"Forget it," he said. "Fly to Siberia *immediately*. I'll send you the exact coordinates in a moment, along with a packet of instructions and Aurora Beatrix Lane's diary."

"**SIBERIA**?" asked Cassidy, dumbfounded. "Irina Lenenko told us to go there?"

"Thanks to your incompetent employees, the doctor didn't tell us anything," Luke von Klawitz replied angrily. "I'm calling the shots now, and I'm telling you to get to Siberia."

"Of course, sir," Cassidy replied. "I'll leave immediately."

Just before he hung up, Klawitz added one warning.

"Those five meddling mice will be there," he said. "This time, make sure they don't get in your way. If they do, there will be **trouble** for you, too."

SIBERIAN HOSPITALITY

In Russia, the Thea Sisters and Sergei prepared for their journey to Siberia, unaware that Klawitz knew where they were headed. Once their plane landed, they headed for the airport **EXIT**.

"We'll have to get a taxi to take us to the old country house," Paulina said.

Sergei **shook** his head, smiling.

"No, I asked a friend to meet us," he said.

"Sergei, I'm here!" a cheerful voice called. A mouse was waiting to greet the group at the arrivals entrance.

"**Roman!**" Sergei exclaimed. "How **GREAT** to see you!

"These are my friends, the Thea Sisters:

Paulina, Nicky, Colette, Violet, and Pam."

"**WELCOME** to Siberia," he said. "I came as soon as Seryozha called me."

"Seryozha?" Paulina asked, confused.

"It's a nickname for Sergei," Roman replied, smiling. "I would love to have you over to my house for a quick lunch before you get back to your ʈrɑvels. What do you say?"

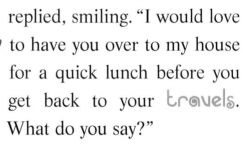

Seryozha!

"That's a great idea!" Pam replied enthusiastically.

Roman lived near the center of the city. He parked a few steps from a building with elegant columns.

"What is that?" asked Colette.

"It's the opera house,"

Roman replied. "The next time you come, I will take you all to see a **ballet** there!"

Pam was about to reply, when she was startled by the sound of a car engine starting.

"That car started by itself!" she squeaked in surprise. "But how? There's no one inside!"

Roman and Sergei exchanged a look and exploded with laughter.

"Here in Siberia, it's so cold that many people have remote starters for their cars," Sergei explained. "This prevents the motor from freezing if it hasn't been running recently."

"In the worst part of winter, the temperatures can go down to **NEGATIVE FIFTY DEGREES**!" Roman added.

"What?!" Paulina exclaimed in surprise. "But how do you survive?"

"We dress very warmly, wear HEAVY scarves, and keep our houses well heated," Roman said. "Speaking of houses, here's mine!"

As soon as they entered the home, the Thea Sisters removed their shoes and went into the living room, where they were immediately enveloped in a cozy warmth.

"The houses really *are* well heated," Violet commented, her cheeks flushed from the heat.

"I told you," Roman said, smiling. Then he led them to the table in the dining room, where he had already set out some soup, currant juice, fresh fruit, and a yummy-looking dessert.

"I love Russian hospitality!" Pam squeaked happily.

"Unfortunately, I can't come with you to

the country," Roman told them. "But I would be happy to loan you my car. You can bring it back whenever you're done."

"Thank you!" Paulina said. "That's so kind. It's wonderful to be able to have friends we can count on all **around the world**!"

SAINT PETERSBURG

MOSCOW

RUSSIA

NOVOSIBIRSK

A LUCKY TUMBLE

When they were finished with lunch, the group thanked Roman and said good-bye. After a forty-five-minute car ride, they arrived at the place Irina had told them about.

"According to the map, Hannah's husband's family home must be down there!" Nicky exclaimed, pointing to the other side of the river.

"But how do we **get there**?" Paulina asked, confused.

"By foot!" Sergei responded, smiling. "Don't worry: It's **frozen** solid and completely safe."

To demonstrate, he walked down to the edge of the river and stepped out onto the

icy surface. The Thea Sisters followed behind him, hesitantly at first. Ice can be very dangerous and should never be crossed alone!

Once they realized how firm the surface was, they **RELAXED**. A few minutes later, the group was standing on the other side of the river in front of a small **WOODEN** building covered in **snow**.

A white hare poked out of a bush and **HOPPED** away.

Violet approached the house and noticed that the wooden decorations on the roof and window looked battered and **WORN**.

"I'm not sure anyone lives here anymore," she said.

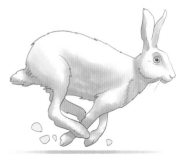

Sergei knocked on the door gently and it swung open.

"You're right," he told Violet. "This cottage has been abandoned."

The group entered. Though it was chilly inside, the wooden hut had a welcoming feeling.

"Do you really think we'll find the queen's jewel here?" Sergei asked, looking around.

"I certainly wouldn't have hidden a precious gem in a place like this!" Colette said as she shivered in the cold. "I pictured some sort of SAFE or a treasure chest worthy of a great queen's jewels!"

BAM!

"Ouch!" Sergei cried as he fell to the floor.

"Are you okay?" Paulina asked in alarm. "What happened?"

"I'm fine," Sergei groaned as he stood up. "I tripped over a loose floor board."

"We need to be careful," Paulina reminded everyone. "It wouldn't be easy to find a doctor out here in the middle of the snow!"

"Look!" Nicky exclaimed, pointing at the wooden floorboard Sergei had tripped over. "I think there's something **under** there!"

"Do you think Aurora hid the jewel under the floorboards?" Colette asked, aghast.

Ouch . . .

"Let's find out!" Nicky said as she pulled a metal box out from the hole beneath the flooring. She opened the box.

"I'm sorry to disappoint you, Coco, but it's only an old, yellowed piece of paper . . ."

"But that's *Aurora's* handwriting!" Colette said, taking the paper in her paws. Then she began to read . . .

It shines ever green and bright,
Even on the darkest night.
A famouse queen wore it on her head,
As word of her enchanting beauty spread.
Before the asp took its fatal bite,
She hid the jewel out of sight.
In a desert flat and white,
Hides this gem of precious light.

A SiNiSTER SURPRiSE

"Wow," Paulina murmured. "Aurora always keeps us on our paws! Just when we thought we had found an answer, she surprises us with a new puzzle!"

Violet smiled. "It was the only way she could protect her discoveries from the greedy Jan von Klawitz," she said.

"Well, at least this time the riddle seems easy," Violet said.

"It does?" Pam replied, a puzzled look on her snout.

Violet nodded. "It mentions a famouse queen with enchanting beauty," she explained. "Then there's the part about an asp taking a fatal bite. An asp is a snake . . .

it's definitely about Cleopatra, the powerful **queen of ancient Egypt**!

"She was famouse for her great beauty, and according to legend, she died from a snake bite."

"I have a pretty good guess as to what type of gem we're looking for, too," Colette said. She pointed to the small pendant around her neck. "The poem says, 'It shines ever **green** and bright.' I'm sure it's an **EMERALD**!"

Pam clapped her paws **happily**. "Now," she began, "all we need to do is . . ."

"All you need to do is listen to us!" a sharp voice said suddenly.

Everyone turned toward the door.

Cassidy had appeared out of **nowhere**. Before Sergei and the Thea Sisters could react, she dashed into the cottage and grabbed the **paper** from Colette's paws and quickly turned to go. In all the commotion, Cassidy dropped her purse.

The others raced outside after her, but she had already scampered across the ice and leaped onto a waiting snowmobile.

Cassidy started up the engine and disappeared into the **snowy** landscape.

"Oh no!" Sergei said bitterly. "She got away again!"

"**Don't worry**," Nicky said reassuringly. "We already read the message, and look what I have here."

Nicky showed everyone Cassidy's purse. Inside was a worn notebook. Paulina took a step closer and got a closer look at it, her eyes growing large.

Ha, ha, ha!

"It's one of Aurora's diaries!" Nicky replied, smiling.

"Incredible!" Colette squeaked. "Klawitz must have gotten his paws on it somehow. That must be how he knew about the queen's jewel!"

"Yes, but a few key pieces of information were missing," Violet said, putting together the pieces of the puzzle. "That's why he mousenapped Irina. He was hoping she would help him fill in the gaps."

"So, although we lost Aurora's clue, we know it refers to the famouse queen Cleopatra," Nicky recapped.

"Yes, and we can assume she hid the emerald in the Sahara," Violet added.

"Really?" Paulina said. "How?"

"Well, the poem mentions 'a desert flat and white,'" Violet pointed out. "And since

Cleopatra was the queen of Egypt, it must be the Sahara! And now that we also have *Aurora's* diary, we should be able to put together the rest of the clues."

"Let's head back to the airport," Pam suggested. "On the way, we can read the diary and figure out our NEXT STEPS."

"Perfect!" Colette squeaked. "Let's go!"

SAHARA DESERT + CLEOPATRA = THE QUEEN'S JEWEL

?N EGYPT!

A few hours later, the Thea Sisters were taking their seats aboard a plane to Egypt.

"I still can't believe Cassidy stole that clue," Pam said, sighing. "Everything just happened so fast!"

"Don't worry about it, Pam," Colette told her reassuringly.

"It's true, it's good she showed up. We gained more than we lost!" Paulina agreed. "And thanks to Aurora's diary, we know exactly where in the Egyptian desert we need to go."

"Yes, let's go over it again just to be sure," Pam said.

Colette **smiled** and opened the notebook.

Dear Diary,

I will never get tired of the feeling I get when I make a new discovery after a long, difficult search. It's exhilarating! It's even more special in a case like this one, when it's a truly precious and *irreplaceable treasure.*

But it is also a huge responsibility. Each artifact needs to be preserved and protected from the greedy paws of unscrupulous mice like Jan von Klawitz.

So I have decided to keep this surprising new treasure carefully hidden until I am certain it will end up in trustworthy paws. Eventually, I want it to be made public so it can be treasured and admired by mice all around the globe. But until then, I will leave the queen's jewel in the desert. The star compass will lead to an expanse that's pure and white.

Colette turned to Paulina and Sergei.

"Thank goodness you were able to figure out the **exact** location based on Aurora's cryptic clues!" she said.

Sergei smiled. "We had to do a little research, but when we learned there are five oases in the vast area known as the **White Desert**, we knew we had found it!"

"And Aurora writes about a 'star compass,' because the best way to navigate in the desert is by using the **stars** like a **compass**," Paulina added. "The five oases are Kharga, Dakhla, Farafra, Bahariya, and Siwa. There is a point between Bahariya and Siwa where the sand is as white as snow and there are unusual calcium rock formations that tower over the landscape."

"An expanse that's pure and white,"

Colette murmured, repeating the words from Aurora's diary.

"The area is popular with tourists because the rock formations and the sand are so unique," Paulina said.

"And you think a jewel is buried near there?" Pam asked. "And this jewel used to belong to Cleopatra, right?"

"Exactly!" Violet confirmed, smiling.

"While we were looking for information about the area, we discovered that there is a natural spring in the Siwa Oasis that the Egyptian queen loved to visit," Colette continued. "It's called Cleopatra's Pool."

"So there's a pretty good chance the

emerald is hidden there?" Nicky asked.

Colette nodded.

"Yes, I think that's likely," she confirmed. "We should start our search in Siwa."

"Let's hope we can find it," Nicky said, a worried look on her snout. "Cleopatra was extremely *intelligent* and cunning. She wouldn't hide a precious jewel just anywhere. She would be sure the spot was well hidden and very **difficult** to find."

THE LAST PHARAOH OF EGYPT

"I have an idea!" Paulina said. "In my Egypt **guidebook**, there's a section dedicated to the life of Cleopatra. Let's read it and see if there are any clues that might help us track down the treasure."

Let's read the guide!

Cleopatra, the Last Pharaoh of Ancient Egypt

Cleopatra VII Philopator was the most famouse queen in Egyptian history. Born in Alexandria, Egypt, around 69 BC, Cleopatra was the daughter of Pharaoh Ptolemy XII. When her father died in 51 BC, eighteen-year-old Cleopatra and her ten-year-old brother, Ptolemy XIII, took the throne and ruled together until her brother pushed her into exile in 49 BC.

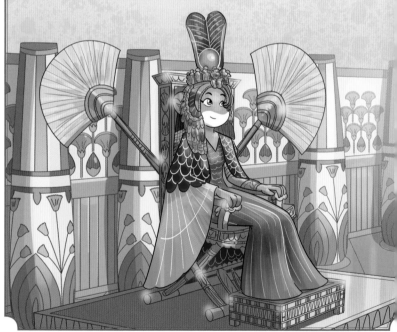

While in exile, Cleopatra gathered an army, turning to the Roman dictator Julius Caesar for help. She then returned to Egypt, defeated her brother Ptolemy XIII, and was reinstalled as queen. In 47 BC, Cleopatra and Caesar had a son, Caesarion (meaning "Little Caesar").

Cleopatra traveled to Rome with Caesar, but after his death in 44 BC, she returned to Egypt to rule as queen. A power struggle continued in Rome, but by 42 BC, Rome was in the hands of Roman general Mark Antony and Caesar's adopted son Octavian.

Soon afterward, Mark Antony and Cleopatra met, and the couple fell in love and had three children together. Egypt continued to prosper under Cleopatra, and Mark Antony returned portions of Egypt's eastern empire that had been under Roman rule to Cleopatra.

Worried by Cleopatra's power in Egypt, Octavian declared war on the queen in 32 BC and proclaimed Mark Antony a traitor to Rome. Later that year, Octavian's forces defeated Mark Antony and Cleopatra.

When the Thea Sisters and Sergei had finished reading about Cleopatra's life, they were suddenly overwhelmed with exhaustion from their many adventures. The six friends soon fell asleep.

When the plane finally landed in Cairo,

the Thea Sisters and Sergei awoke feeling refreshed and ready for their next CHALLENGE. They stepped off the airplane and into the warm Egyptian air.

"This heat feels amazing after Siberia!" Pam said happily. "It's like going from the fridge to the oven! Speaking of ovens . . ."

"Let me guess," Sergei said playfully. "You're ready for a snack, right?"

"Of course!" Pam exclaimed. "What better way to get to know a new place than through its cuisine?"

Pam winked at her friends, who all laughed.

"Can you at least wait until we get into the city, Pam?" Paulina asked. "As soon as we get checked into the hotel, we'll find a restaurant nearby."

The group quickly claimed their backpacks

and luggage and headed out of the airport terminal.

"There's the **BUS** stop," Violet said, pointing.

"Let's go!" Colette said eagerly. "The faster we get to the hotel, the faster we can plan our excursion to the desert!"

Sergei and the Thea Sisters hopped on the bus, excited for their next adventure. But none of them realized that Cassidy had been hidden behind some palm trees in the terminal, watching their every move.

LURKING IN THE SHADOWS

While the Thea Sisters and Sergei arrived in Egypt, Luke von Klawitz was hidden deep under the ice in his underground lab in Alaska. Klawitz had been spending many hours there, plotting evil, twirling his mustache, hunched over a table piled with papers, maps, and documents. Nearby, images of archaeological **ARTIFACTS** scrolled across a large screen.

Suddenly, a loud ring from his wrist communicator made Klawitz JUMP UP in surprise.

"Yes, Cassidy," he squeaked, annoyed. "What is it? I thought I told you not to disturb me."

Cassidy's **smiling** snout appeared on the large SCREEN.

"Yes, I know, but I have something important to tell you," Cassidy squeaked excitedly.

"Well, what is it?" Klawitz demanded impatiently.

I told you not to disturb me!

It took Cassidy a moment to regain her composure. She hadn't expected her boss to be so **irritable**.

"As you know, we discovered that Queen Cleopatra's jewel is probably hidden in the Sahara Desert," she said. "But until now, we weren't sure exactly where to search."

"So you bothered me to tell me things I already know?" Klawitz replied **SCORNFULLY**. "Get to the point!"

"Yes, of course," Cassidy continued. "At the Cairo airport I came across the mice from Mouseford. I eavesdropped on them, and it seems they've figured out where to look for the jewel."

"**WHERE?**" Klawitz asked eagerly.

"I don't know," Cassidy admitted. "But I'm sure we'll figure it out soon."

"Very interesting," Klawitz murmured as

he stroked his beard thoughtfully.

"They must have noticed something in Aurora's **diary** that you fools missed! But now we'll use their knowledge *against* them."

Klawitz threw back his head and began to laugh.

"Ha, ha, ha, ha, ha, ha, ha, ha, ha!"

Cassidy was taken aback by his response. "Um, sir, is everything okay?" she asked timidly.

"Yes," he snarled. "Everything is just perfect. Get back to work!"

And with that, he disconnected their communication, and the screen in front of him went **DARK**.

"Those five mice think they're so smart," Luke von Klawitz hissed under his breath as he continued to stare at the black screen. "They don't have any idea who they're dealing with, but they're about to **FIND OUT**!"

LUCK AT THE MARKET

In Cairo, a whirl of ńǫises, COLORS, and aromas enveloped Sergei and the Thea Sisters. All around them they could hear the clamor of passersby mixed with the

blaring car horns and the loud calls of shop owners.

"Here's our hotel!" Paulina announced.

Sergei went to his room to unpack and freshen up while the Thea Sisters settled into their own space.

"I would love to take a little nap!" Violet exclaimed as she threw herself down on the bed.

"I'm afraid we don't have much time to relax," Nicky said. "If we're going to head to the desert tomorrow, we have to go buy some water, sunscreen, hats, and some heavy blankets to keep us warm at night."

Hats . . .

"And don't forget that it's almost dinnertime," Pam warned. "You don't want to drag me around shopping on an EMPTY STOMACH!"

"Don't worry, Pam," Paulina reassured her. "I have a place for shopping and eating: Khan el-Khalili. It's an open-air bazaar full of unique items including food, spices, jewelry, and clothes."

"That sounds perfect!" Violet exclaimed.

A short while later, Sergei joined them and the friends found themselves at the entrance to the bazaar.

"Wow!" Pam exclaimed, dazed by the many mice and goods crammed inside the colorful market.

The group dove into the labyrinth of tight alleys, which were full of unique objects and tempting aromas.

Nicky and Sergei stopped to buy large water bottles, while Colette couldn't resist a stop at a perfume stall to try a few fragrances.

Violet was studying an array of musical instruments she had never seen before, while Paulina bought an amber bracelet for her sister, Maria. Pam was drawn to a stall full of delicious-smelling foods, where she

KHAN EL-KHALILI

The oldest open-air market in the Middle East, Khan El-Khalili has been in operation since the 1300s. At one time the market was known as a place to buy and trade silk and jewels. Today, the market is famouse for its clothing, spices, jewelry, perfume, carpets, souvenirs, crafts, and much more.

ordered dinner for everyone.

"I'll take some falafel," she told the mouse in the stall, **pointing** at one dish. "And some *ful mudammas, koshari, aish baladi.*"

"Is that all?" asked the merchant.

"Ah, no," Pam said. "I'll also have some *torshi*, and baklava for dessert, please!"

While she was waiting for her order, Pam started snacking on some of the falafel.

"Mmmm," she murmured to herself. "These are delicious. I think I'll get some more . . ."

As the merchant handed Pam three bags full of CONTAINERS, she heard a warm laugh behind her.

"I hope this isn't all just for you!" a friendly voice teased.

When Pam turned, she saw a mouse with dark hair and **kind** eyes in line behind her.

"Um . . . it's for my friends as well," Pam explained hurriedly. "But maybe I got too much."

"No, excuse me," the mouse apologized. "I was only joking. I'm so glad you appreciate delicious food!"

The boy turned to the vendor and smiled.

"Amir, for me, the usual," he said.

The vendor quickly served the mouse a **falafel** wrap.

A TASTE OF EGYPT

★ *Falafel:* deep-fried balls made from ground fava beans or chickpeas

★ *Ful mudammas:* fava beans stewed with tahini and seasoned with garlic, cumin, and lemon

★ *Koshari:* spiced lentils and rice, chickpeas, pasta, fried onions, and tomato sauce

★ *Aish baladi:* flatbread made with whole-wheat flour

★ *Torshi:* pickled vegetables

★ *Baklava:* dessert of phyllo dough filled with nuts, honey, and dried fruit

"My name is Omar," the boy said, introducing himself to Pam.

"Hi," she replied. "I'm Pam."

"Did I hear correctly that you're going to the desert tomorrow?" Omar asked.

"Oh yes," Pam replied. "My FRIENDS and I want to visit Cleopatra's Pool."

The boy brightened.

"Oh, you made a great choice," he replied. "It's a wonderful trip! I hope you reserved a good guide."

"Actually, we still need to FIND one," Pam admitted.

"Well it's really your lucky day!" he said. "I happen to be the best guide for desert excursions. I study archaeology at Oxford University, but every summer I come back to Egypt, where my grandmother lives. I work as a guide right in the area you're planning to visit. If you want, I would be happy to accompany you and your friends."

A moment later, Nicky, Sergei, Violet, Paulina, and Colette appeared.

"Hi!" Pam greeted her friends. "I was just getting us something to eat. And I also happened to meet someone who can HELP us. This is Omar. He works as a guide in the desert."

"That's great NEWS!" Colette exclaimed, clapping her paws. "Can you take us to Siwa tomorrow?"

"Definitely," Omar said. "But you won't be able to visit Cleopatra's Pool until the day after that."

"But why?" Violet asked, a confused look on her snout.

"The fastest way to get to the Siwa Oasis is to pass through the town of Marsa

Matruh on the northern coast," Omar explained. "The trip takes more than eight hours, and I recommend you make a few stops before you arrive in Siwa in the evening. The trip is a long one, but I think you'll really like the coast."

The Thea Sisters, Sergei, and Omar decided on a time and place to meet early the following morning.

"See you then!" Omar said as he waved good-bye. "A beautiful adventure awaits us tomorrow!"

SAND AND MORE SAND

The next day, the alarm clock rang at 6 a.m. on the dot.

"Oh no!" Violet exclaimed. She buried her head in the pillow. "Don't tell me it's already time to **get up**!"

"Yes!" Nicky said enthusiastically. "We have just enough time to get ready and have **breakfast** before we have to meet Omar."

"Sleeping bag, flashlight, compass, fleece . . . Did we pack everything?" Colette asked **sleepily**.

"I would say so," Nicky replied.

Sergei was waiting for the Thea Sisters

outside his room. The group ate a filling breakfast and then headed out to meet their new friend. Omar was waiting for them in his **SUV**.

Omar began to drive, and as soon as they left the city, he gave them some background on the area they were headed to.

"The Siwa Oasis is a remarkable fertile basin in the middle of the Sahara Desert's Great Sand Sea," Omar explained. "The area is full of small, clear lakes and springs and is rich with palms and olive trees."

As Omar spoke, the Thea Sisters watched the landscape scroll by. Along the coast, palm trees soared up toward the sky as WAVES crashed against the rocky shore, creating sparkling splashes of foam.

After a few hours of driving, Omar parked the car near the coast.

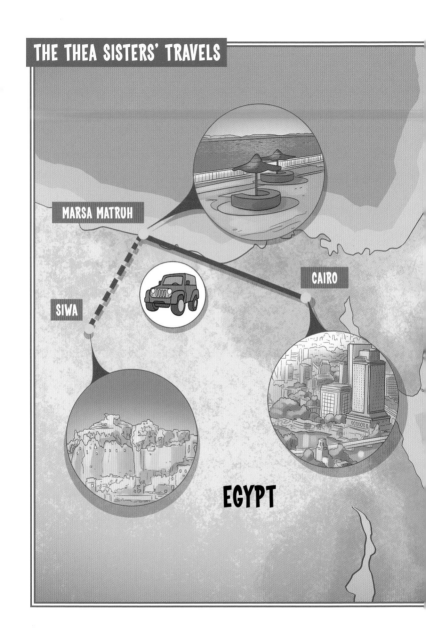

THE THEA SISTERS' TRAVELS

MARSA MATRUH

SIWA

CAIRO

EGYPT

"We are in the city of Marsa Matruh!" he announced. "We'll stop here for lunch and to stretch our legs. Then we'll leave the coast and head deep into the heart of the desert. So use this time to eat at a good restaurant and make any last purchases before we head for the oasis!"

Nicky couldn't wait to get out in the open air. She leaped out of the SUV first, followed by Sergei and the rest of her friends. Everyone walked together toward the center of town, where they got sandwiches to take to the beach for a picnic lunch.

"What a beautiful landscape," Nicky exclaimed as she turned toward the sea, taking deep breaths of the fresh, salty air.

Omar nodded.

"Enjoy the water, because in the desert, we'll see nothing but sand!"

After they finished lunch, Sergei and Paulina took a walk on the beach, while Nicky went for a short **JOG**. Violet and Pam took a nap, Colette flipped through the guidebook of Egypt, and Omar went to check on the car.

After an hour, Colette went back to the car, too. She had some questions for Omar about their destination.

"Omar, how long has Cleopatra's Pool been in Siwa?" Colette asked. "And is the original . . . oh, sorry!"

She suddenly realized her friend was talking on the **phone**.

". . . we'll get there tonight and tomorrow we can explore," Omar was saying. When he saw Colette, he cut it short. "I need to go now, **GRANDMA**. We'll chat soon!

"That was my grandma," he explained,

smiling. "I was letting her know my cell phone still works here.

"She worries about me a lot, especially now that she is older. We should really get going. Let's call the others!"

Colette went to tell the other Thea Sisters and Sergei that it was time to go. Soon everyone was back in the SUV and the group was on the road again. In just a few minutes, the **landscape** around them changed completely. Suddenly, the only thing on the horizon was the long gray ribbon of the road ahead. Around them it was just **sand** and **more sand** . . .

"It feels like the city is light-years away," Nicky said.

"The desert is a powerful place," Omar said. "It's one of those places that makes you realize how big our world really is."

The rest of the trip passed *quietly*. Sergei and the Thea Sisters napped and watched the miles of sand pass by, each lost in their own **thoughts**.

The sun was beginning to set when Paulina spotted something.

"Look!" she squeaked, pointing at the horizon.

Ahead of them was a large BUTTRESS of rock, encircled at the base by a forest of palm trees and some huts.

"We have arrived at Siwa Oasis!" Omar announced.

THE SIWA OASIS

Siwa sits about sixty feet below sea level. The oasis has a population of around 30,000 people and is one of Egypt's most isolated settlements. Olive, palm, and date trees thrive in the area, which is known for its clear spring water. Three famouse stops in Siwa are the Temple of the Oracle, the Temple of Amun, and Cleopatra's Pool.

THE EMERALD OF ETERNAL BEAUTY

Sergei, Omar, and the Thea Sisters got out of the car in front of a building surrounded by TALL PALM TREES and green shrubs.

"Wow!" Pam exclaimed. "A minute ago, all around us was sand as far as the eye could see. Where did all this VEGETATION come from?!"

"That is how oases are: unexpected and almost unbelievable!" Omar said, smiling.

The Thea Sisters looked around in awe. After many hours in the car staring out at nothing but sand, the green around them made them feel unexpectedly joyful. In the distance, the rays of the setting sun gave the landscape a pink-and-orange glow.

"I reserved a room in this inn," Omar said. The place was modest but had everything one could want after a long **trip** through the desert. Sergei and the Thea Sisters headed to their rooms to **relax** a bit before dinner.

"Egypt is such a lovely country, full of **delicious** dishes!"

We'll stay here!

Pam exclaimed as she tasted a few local dates.

The Thea Sisters enjoyed dinner. They were excited to be so close to Cleopatra's Pool.

"Now I have to say good night," Omar told them, excusing himself at the end of the meal. "I need to call my grandma before I go to sleep. Tomorrow morning, we will head straight to Cleopatra's Pool. Remember to bring **HATS**, scarves, and sunscreen to protect your fur from the wind and sun."

"Good night!" Paulina told Omar. Then she turned to Sergei. "We should have everything we need for tomorrow. Colette packed extra supplies for everyone, right Coco?"

But Colette didn't reply. She was looking at something on the wall in front of her.

"Look!" she exclaimed, pointing. "Am I mistaken, or is that Cleopatra?"

The Thea Sisters turned to look at the painting, which hung on the wall near their dinner table. The scene depicted the queen of Egypt. But the most remarkable thing about the painting was the CROWN on Cleopatra's head. In its center was an enormouse green emerald!

In an instant the six mice were huddled at the wall. Pam PUSHED ASIDE a curtain that covered part of the image to reveal four scenes that featured

Cleopatra and the fabumouse jewel.

"I see that you are interested in the legend of the **EMERALD OF ETERNAL BEAUTY**!" exclaimed a mouse sitting nearby. He rose from his seat and approached them.

"The emerald of eternal beauty?" Colette repeated.

"It's a famous legend tied to Queen Cleopatra," the mouse explained.

"Could you tell us about it?" Sergei asked.

"Of course," he said. "It's a pleasure finding young mice who are interested in ancient history. You see, I'm a history professor."

"We're actually very interested in the life of Cleopatra," Colette said.

"Then you know she was a very **FASCINATING RODENT**," the professor continued. "According to the legend, Cleopatra received a very precious emerald as a gift from one of her admirers.

"It was said that the mouse who possessed the jewel would have beauty that would never fade. The queen had the gem placed in a crown that she wore at all times.

"Cleopatra was convinced that the gem had immense power. In fact, she was so worried one of her enemies would try to steal it that she hid the jewel and didn't tell anyone where it was! As a result, the famous jewel was lost when the queen died."

"What are these symbols?" Paulina asked, pointing at some hieroglyphics near the design on the wall.

"That's the most *interesting* part of the legend," the professor replied. "When Cleopatra hid the emerald, she left a dedication to the god Ra:

"At the beginning of the Spring, turn to where Ra appears,

"Then give him fifteen scepters, and bow down when he nears."

Sergei and the Thea Sisters couldn't **believe** their ears. Were those directions to the jewel's hiding place?

The professor saw their expressions and laughed.

"It's only a legend," he said, smiling. "No need to take it so seriously."

But the Thea Sisters knew that sometimes **LEGENDS** were more real than they seemed . . .

AT CLEOPATRA'S POOL

The following morning, the Thea Sisters and Sergei met Omar before dawn at the entrance to the inn. After a quick breakfast, they set off for Cleopatra's Pool.

But instead of going in the SUV as they had expected, they found a wooden cart strapped to a donkey waiting for them in front of the inn.

"This is Ziki," Omar announced, pointing at the animal. "He will take us to Cleopatra's Pool!"

"Really?!" Violet asked in surprise.

Omar nodded, smiling.

"Donkeys are the local means of

Really?!

transportation," he explained. "It will be a terrific ride. You'll see!"

The Thea Sisters and Sergei got in the cart. Omar climbed into the driver's seat, and they were off. Before long, the cart pulled up in front of a large pool of **emerald** water. On one side, they saw some small shops selling **COLORFUL** carpets, a bar selling fruit juices, and a bike rental shop.

The sun was still low in the sky and the area around the pool was quiet and free of tourists.

"Now where do we begin?" Pam asked, scratching her head.

"Well, you can relax and have a fresh juice at the bar," Omar began. "Or maybe you want to take a swim."

The friends exchanged a look: Could they trust their new friend enough to tell him the real reason for their visit? The Thea Sisters glanced at Sergei. They had trusted him, after all. Perhaps it was time to let Omar in on their **SECRET MISSION** as well.

"We asked you to bring us here because we're looking for something special," Paulina explained. "A precious jewel, to be exact."

"A jewel?" Omar asked. "Which jewel?"

"THE EMERALD OF ETERNAL BEAUTY," Colette replied.

"But that's a legend for tourists!" Omar replied, laughing.

"We have reason to believe it's much more than that," Pam explained. "And we think the jewel could be hidden nearby."

"Really?!" Omar exclaimed, suddenly becoming serious.

"Well, we're not certain," Nicky said. "But we think it might be here."

"Do you have some sort of **proof**?" Omar prodded them.

"Not exactly," Violet said. "I think we should split into two groups and look around a bit."

The Thea Sisters and Sergei separated and searched the area around the pool while Omar WATCHED them from a distance.

When the two groups met up again, they hadn't found a thing. Sergei and the Thea Sisters flopped down at the edge of the pool, disheartened.

"It looks like our search has come to a dead end," Pam said with a sigh.

WHERE RA APPEARS

"Come on, now," Omar said **encouragingly**. "Don't look so down in the snouts. Why don't we go over the clues?"

Paulina shook her head.

"It's pointless," she said. "We've been through it a **thousand** times. That was our last clue to the location of the emerald of eternal beauty."

"The emerald of eternal beauty," echoed Nicky. "That's it! I found the key! We found it yesterday!"

"We learned the legend of the emerald at the restaurant," Colette said. "But there weren't any clues to the **location** of the jewel in the images."

"No, not in the images, but in the text!" Nicky said excitedly. "The dedication to the god Ra sounded like directions, didn't it? Sergei, you wrote it down, right?"

It's a clue!

Sergei flipped through the pages of his notebook.

"Here it is!" he shouted. "The dedication reads: *At the beginning of the Spring, turn to where Ra appears, then give him fifteen scepters, and bow down when he nears.*"

"That doesn't seem like a **clue**," Omar remarked.

"But it does!" Nicky exclaimed. "Think about it: Ra is the god associated with the sun. Where does Ra appear?"

"The east!" Sergei replied.

"Exactly!" Nicky exclaimed. "And maybe the beginning of spring isn't the season, but the entrance to Cleopatra's Pool, which is a type of spring!"

"So if we stand at the entrance to the pool, we should turn **east**," Violet said.

"And the part about scepters?" Pam asked.

"An ANTIQUE Egyptian scepter was about the length of an arm," Omar explained. "That would be about one pawstep!"

THE SOLUTION TO THE RIDDLE:

At the beginning of the Spring = At the entrance to the pool

turn to where Ra appears = look east

then give him fifteen scepters = take fifteen steps

and bow down when he nears = and look low

"That means we take fifteen steps to the east," Colette said. "And then we bow down and look low. We solved the RIDDLE!"

"It's definitely worth a try," Colette said.

The Thea Sisters and Omar went to the entrance to the pool, turned east, took fifteen steps, and stopped right in front of a rock with two TALL PALM TREES right behind it.

"We have to dig here," Sergei said. "Omar, do you have something we could use?"

"Sure," Omar said, and he pulled out a small shovel from his backpack.

Sergei stooped down and began to dig in the sand. Suddenly, the shovel hit something hard.

"It's . . . it's a chest!" he exclaimed, pulling out a small stone coffer.

"The treasure!" Omar exclaimed. "The queen's treasure! You really found it!"

"Incredible," Colette whispered.

"Nice work," came a **cold** voice behind them.

When the Thea Sisters and Sergei turned, the smiles on their snouts disappeared. It was Stan and Max!

"Now HAND IT OVER," Stan said menacingly. "Or else."

A BITTER
SURPRISE

The THEA SiSTERS looked at each other in shock. How had Luke von Klawitz's **accomplices** followed them there?

"Give us the treasure," Max said.

Give us the treasure!

"We're not going to give you anything!" Colette cried. "This treasure is not yours to take. And there are **seven** of us against you **TWO**!"

Stan just laughed.

"Right, and you're going to get away on what?" he scoffed. "That little donkey?"

Suddenly, it dawned on the Thea Sisters

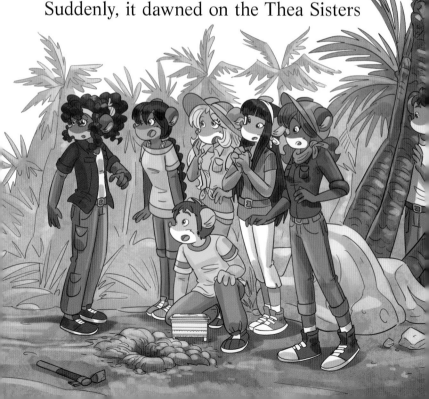

that he was right. There was no way for them to get away.

"We're not going to give up so easily!" Nicky said boldly, **holding** the treasure tightly. Then she glanced at Pam and gave a subtle nod of her head.

Pam took a few steps **closer** to Nicky.

"What are you waiting for?" Stan said to

I got it!

Huh?!

Take it!

Max as he pointed at Nicky. "Go take it from her!"

But just as Max was about to reach her, Nicky threw the CHEST in the air.

"Pam, catch it!" she called.

"Got it!" Pam exclaimed, grabbing the precious treasure in her two paws and running in the OPPOSITE DIRECTION.

Sergei then ran to the side, just in time for Pam to pass him the chest.

But as soon as he turned to escape, Sergei found himself snout to snout with Stan, who snatched the chest from his paws.

"Finally!" Stan exclaimed in relief. "We have Cleopatra's treasure in our paws!"

He QUICKLY opened the chest.

"The queen's emerald!"

Inside was a gold crown with a large, brilliant green emerald nestled in the center.

Excited, Stan reached in to pull it out. But as soon as his paw touched it, he realized something wasn't right. In an instant, the jewel began to **crumble** into a dusty powder, turning his paw green.

"But wh-what?!" he **stuttered** in surprise.

The crown broke in half, and one part fell on the ground in the sand.

Sergei jumped up and grabbed it.

"It's salt," he said, licking his paw. "This crown is made of salt! And the emerald is salt that's been **colored** green!"

"Th-that's impossible!" Max said, suddenly looking afraid. "Who will tell Klawitz that we've failed again?"

"We followed the wrong clue," Stan said. Then he turned ANGRILY toward Sergei and the Thea Sisters. "It's your fault . . . You did this on purpose!"

"Let it be," Max said, grabbing his partner by the sleeve. "Let's not **waste** any more time here."

"You're right. Let's go," Stan replied. But he shook his paw menacingly at the young mice. "This doesn't end here. We'll find that emerald, and we're not going to let you get in our way!"

The two left quickly, dropping the chest in the sand.

"Oh, that was **awful**!" Nicky squeaked, burying her snout in her paws.

"Yes, but we're all fine and that's the most important thing," Colette said.

"Yes, but where is Omar?" Sergei asked.

They all looked around, but no one saw the mouse anywhere.

"Omar!" Nicky called out. "Omar?!"

There was no reply. Around them, the desert was **silent**.

"Do you think something happened to him?" Pam asked.

"Let's try calling him," Sergei said. But he soon found that Omar's cell phone had been turned off.

"Now what do we do?" asked Pam, looking at her friends in **dismay**.

RETURNING WITH EMPTY PAWS

The Thea Sisters and Sergei thought quietly for a moment, feeling discouraged. Where could Omar have gone?

"I'll send him a text!" Paulina said. She pulled out her **phone** and typed a message to Omar.

The *sun* had risen completely by now, and the first tourists were beginning to arrive to admire Cleopatra's Pool.

Colette had picked up the chest and was examining it more closely.

"Hey, look at this!" she said, extracting a yellowed piece of folded paper from the bottom of the chest.

"It's a note. Listen to this . . ."

Dear explorer,

You have come so far. I don't know if you are a friend of truth and honesty like me, or if you are motivated by greed like my enemy Professor von Klawitz. Either way, you hoped to find the queen's treasure here in the desert and instead you found a pawful of salt. But it isn't meant to be a trick or a joke. The trail you followed was the right one, and the emerald of eternal beauty does exist! I found it right here, in this same chest, after a long search.

But since greedy mice want to get their paws on this wonderful jewel, I was forced to find another hiding place far away from here.

I cannot reveal any more, but if you have a pure heart and an intelligent mind, you will know how to read the hidden clues . . .

Good luck with your search,
Aurora Beatrix Lane

"You will know to read the hidden clues," Violet repeated thoughtfully. "What could that mean?"

"I don't know," Colette said. "But now I think our next move is to return to Cairo."

"Any word from Omar?" Nicky asked Paulina.

"No, nothing," she replied, shaking her head.

"He probably got scared and *TOOK OFF*," Nicky said. "Maybe we can find him back in Cairo."

"I wonder if we can get back there faster than the way we came," Violet said, glancing at the donkey and cart.

"Look," Sergei said. He pointed at an **SUV** that some tourists were getting out of. The driver kept the motor **running**.

"Maybe he's headed back to Siwa. From

there we can look for a ride to Cairo. Let's go ask!"

In no time, the Thea Sisters and Sergei had entrusted the donkey to some mice at the juice bar. Then they caught a ride back to Siwa in the **SUV**. From there, the friends were able to join a busload of tourists heading back to Cairo through the White Desert, with a stop in the Bahariya Oasis.

The six mice found themselves seated near some enthusiastic tourists who were intent on **photographing** every detail of

the desert landscape. Unfortunately, they were unable to enjoy the trip themselves. Instead, they sat in **silence** thinking about what had happened.

Finally, Paulina said what they had all been thinking.

"I just don't understand how **Stan** and **MAX** knew where we were!" she exclaimed, a baffled look on her snout.

"I don't think they could have followed us," Sergei said. "The desert landscape makes it very hard to hide from others. We would have **noticed** them."

"True," Violet agreed. "It seems they knew beforehand where we were headed and when. But **HOW**?"

The friends were quiet as they thought about it. No one had any answers.

"We're not going to solve this **mystery**

THE WHITE DESERT

This vast desert is part of the Sahara. It covers more than one million square miles, from the western banks of the Nile River, west into Libya. The desert includes five oases: Kharga, Dakhla, Farafra, Bahariya, and Siwa. The landscape is covered in dramatic rock formations made of chalk and limestone that have been shaped by the wind.

right now," Nicky finally said with a sigh. "In the meantime, let's try to enjoy the landscape. Look! We're crossing the White Desert."

The friends looked out the window and saw enormouse WHITE BOULDERS in the most unusual shapes dotting the landscape.

"The White Desert . . . Cleopatra," Violet mumbled. "There must be a clue to the treasure's location somewhere. But where?"

A NEW CLUE

Once they were back in Cairo, the **friends** had no way of reaching Omar. They didn't know his last name or his address. The only possible contact for him was Amir, his friend from the food stand in the Khan el-Khalili market. They headed straight to the open-air bazaar.

Have you seen Omar?

No, sorry!

"I haven't seen him. I'm sorry," Amir replied when they asked about

Omar. "But if he comes by, I'll tell him that you were looking for him!"

"This is my **NUMBER**," Pam told Amir. "If you see him, tell him I'm waiting for his call!"

The group exited the market, but they had no idea where to go next.

"**WHAT DO WE DO NOW?**" Nicky asked.

"I think we need to get back to Russia," Violet finally said. "It's almost time for us to head back to Mouseford and Whale Island."

Paulina quickly looked for flights on her phone.

"The next available flight to Moscow leaves in **six hours**," she said.

"How sad to be leaving Egypt without solving the mystery!" Pam said, sighing.

"Very sad," Sergei agreed. "I had hoped to find out more about my great-aunt

Aurora. But I'll text my sister to let her know we're headed back to Moscow."

Sergei

We couldn't find the treasure, so we're coming back to Moscow. See you soon!

"What do you say we take advantage of the hours we still have in Cairo to see the Egyptian Museum?" Violet proposed. "I would really like that!"

"Good idea, Vi!" Nicky said, smiling. "We can console ourselves by admiring treasures of ancient Egypt that were discovered by others."

The friends headed toward Tahrir Square, the location of the Egyptian Museum. On the way, Pam stopped at a falafel stall for a snack.

"Even though we didn't find the treasure,

seeing the Sahara and the White Desert was amazing," Colette remarked.

"The desert was beautiful," Pam agreed, taking a bite of her falafel wrap. "Ugh! This falafel is so salty!"

Suddenly, Violet stopped walking.

"The fake emerald was made of salt," Violet murmured. "And the Sahara isn't the only desert in the world. Oh!"

"Are you okay, Vi?" Colette asked, concerned.

"Oh no," Violet groaned, smacking her forehead with her paw. "I got it all wrong! Do you remember the paper we found in Siberia? Aurora didn't mention the Sahara — she just mentioned 'a desert flat and white.'"

"But that's the Sahara, right?" Colette asked, confused.

Violet shook her head.

"If we think of a sandy desert, yes, it's the Sahara," she explained. "But there are other deserts in the world . . ."

"A desert of salt!" Sergei exclaimed. "The emerald is hidden in a desert of salt!"

Violet nodded. "Aurora didn't make an emerald out of salt by chance . . . It was a **clue**!" she exclaimed.

"The Salar de Uyuni," Paulina said a moment later, **holding up** her cell phone. "The largest salt flat in the world is the Salar de Uyuni in Bolivia."

"Forget about Moscow, we're going to **BOLiVia**!" Nicky cheered.

Sergei

Change of plans: We have another clue! The search continues!

A DESERT OF SALT

After a *long* flight, the Thea Sisters and Sergei arrived in Uyuni, Bolivia, the next evening.

"Colette and I will go reserve a hotel for the NIGHT," Nicky told her friends. "Why don't the rest of you find transportation to the salt desert?"

"Great idea!" Pam agreed. "I think we'll need a good **SUV**. Let's head to the car rental agency!"

A half hour later, the group was in an SUV headed to the hotel.

"We have a little **SURPRISE** for everyone," Colette said. "The hotel Nicky and I reserved is pretty special."

"As long as there's a bed, I'll be happy," Violet said as she let out a huge yawn. "I'm WIPED OUT from all this traveling!"

"Well, I'm curious," Paulina said. "What's the surprise?"

"It has something to do with the place we're going," Nicky replied, her eyes TWINKLING. "Take one guess as to what

material was used to build our hotel."

"Salt?!" Sergei exclaimed, looking perplexed.

"Exactly!" Colette cried. "The Luna Salada Hotel is built out of salt bricks. Even the beds are made of salt!"

"Let's hope the food isn't too salty!" Pam joked, and everyone burst out laughing.

The group finally arrived at the hotel and put their bags in their respective rooms.

"Wow, they're really all made of salt!" Paulina exclaimed, looking at the nightstand and bed in the room she shared with Nicky.

"What do you say to a nice dinner?" Pam suggested as she stuck her head into the room.

"That sounds great," Nicky replied. "And I already reserved a table for us at the HOTEL RESTAURANT!"

The friends headed to the restaurant, which had large windows overlooking the expanse of desert that surrounded the hotel.

"How wonderful," Sergei whispered as he looked out at the clear Bolivian sky, which sparkled with thousands of stars.

"Aurora knew how to pick spectacular hiding places, that's for sure," Violet said as she admired the **extraordinary** landscape.

Pam was the only one distracted from the view by the menu.

"Who wants to share some cuñapés?" she asked her friends.

"What are they?" Colette asked curiously.

Cuñapés

"They're delicious little rolls baked with lots of cheese," Pam explained. "Actually, the more I think about them, the more I realize I don't

have to share an order . . . I'll eat them all myself!"

"They sound great," Nicky said. "I'll have some, too."

"We should also order some sopa de mani, which is a delicious peanut soup," Pam said. "Oh, and some quinoa with vegetables!"

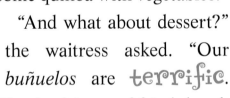

Sopa de mani

"And what about dessert?" the waitress asked. "Our *buñuelos* are terrific. They're fritters of fried dough dusted with powdered sugar."

Buñuelos

"That sounds perfect!" Pam said enthusiastically.

Once the waitress had taken everyone's orders, Sergei and the Thea Sisters began planning.

"Where do you think we should begin our search tomorrow?" Colette asked the others.

"The salt flat is endless," Violet remarked. "*Aurora* must have left us a clue."

"We planned our trip here so **quickly** that we didn't have a chance to read anything about the Salar de Uyuni," Paulina complained.

At that point the waitress returned to the table with their drinks. "Excuse me, but maybe I can **help**!" she said warmly.

227

An Ancient Legend

The waitress sat down next to Nicky.

"My name is Adriana," she said. "I grew up here in Uyuni. The Salar is a very important place for those who live in the area. And it's also very *mysterious*. The salt flat covers more than four thousand square miles and is surrounded by mountains."

"We saw them when we arrived," Nicky said.

"Ah, so you saw **TUNUPA**!"

"Tunupa?" Pam asked, perplexed.

"It's a dormant volcano," Adriana said, smiling. "According to legend, the volcano was once a giant named Tunupa. She married the giant Kusku, but he left her. Tunupa began to cry, and her salty tears formed the Salar."

"What a FASCINATING legend!" Colette said with a sigh.

"Thousands of tourists visit the Salar every year," Adriana continued. "In the RAINY season, a few inches of rain cover the Salar and it becomes an enormouse **mirror**. And in November, three different species of **flamingos** come here to reproduce."

"Wow!" Nicky remarked. "How incredible."

"It is," Adriana agreed. "But it can also be DANGEROUS.

Beware the OJOS DE SALAR, or the Eyes of the Desert!"

"The what?" Sergei asked, a perplexed look on his snout.

"It's another ancient legend," Adriana said playfully. "The story is that the Ojos de Salar would swallow entire caravans as they crossed the desert. But the eyes are really just sinkholes in the ground that fill with water. They can be hard to see in certain light, so you have to be careful."

"This place is full of SURPRISES!" Paulina said.

"Yes, it's true!" Adriana said. "There is

even a cave on Tunupa where you can see three-thousand-year-old mummies. Or you can visit the Isla del Pescado, a rocky hill in the middle of the salt flat that's shaped like a fish and covered in cacti!"

The waitress began to show the group **photographs** of some of the most beautiful places in her country on her phone.

"Bolivia is a spectacular place for those who love **history**, culture, and nature," she explained.

"That's perfect, because we are passionate about all those things!" Violet exclaimed.

"Look here," Adriana said, showing them a photo. "This is Tiwanaku, the most famouse archaeological site in Bolivia. The city was the center of a POWERFUL empire from 500 to 900 AD. It's a beautiful place to visit after a tour of the Salar!"

"We won't have time to stop there," Nicky said. "But we'll have to come back!"

"Tiwanaku is located near the famouse Lake Titicaca," Adriana continued, showing them another photo. "But if you're going to see just one lake in Bolivia, it should be **Laguna Colorada**, located in the Eduardo Avaroa Andean Fauna National Reserve, a bit south of here. Red algae and other microorganisms give the water its unique color."

Adriana flipped to a photo of an unreal-looking **pink-orange** lake.

"Amazing!" Colette exclaimed. "Look at those colors!"

"Speaking of colors, look at these costumes!" Adrianna exclaimed. "This is the Carñaval de Oruro, a festival that happens every year in Oruro."

Tiwanaku

Laguna Colorada

Lake Titicaca

Carnaval de Oruro

The Thea Sisters were crowded around Adriana's phone when someone called out from the kitchen.

"Adriana!"

"Excuse me," the waitress said. "It sounds like I'm needed."

"Of course," Colette said. "You've been so kind, thank you!"

Have a good trip!

"It's nothing," Adrianna replied cheerfully. "Don't forget your hats, sunscreen, and **sunglasses** tomorrow!" she advised before she disappeared into the kitchen.

An Important Decision

Thousands of miles away, in Alaska, Luke von Klawitz waited for updates from his henchmice.

A moment later, there was an incoming call.

"**GOOD MORNING**," squeaked an eager young voice.

"Do you have news for me?" Klawitz barked roughly. "And it had better be useful: **We don't have a moment to lose**."

"After our mission in the Egyptian Sahara failed, I disappeared as you had instructed," the voice continued. "I've been following the Thea Sisters ever since."

"Yes, and?" Klawitz replied **coldly**.

"What have you discovered?"

"Still nothing, I'm afraid," the voice said. "But eventually they will lead us to the jewel."

Klawitz sighed. "They didn't lead us to the treasure in Egypt," he squeaked angrily. "Those **amateur detectives** are incompetent, just like you. You were going to be my secret weapon, but you've just been another miserable failure!"

"Please, sir," came the reply. "I'm asking you to trust me one last time. I'm sure they will lead us to the jewel. I just need a few more days . . ."

"I don't have days to wait!" Klawitz thundered. "Continue to FOLLOW them, but don't call me again unless you discover something interesting."

Klawitz **abruptly** ended the call before

the mouse could respond. Then he immediately placed another call.

"Are you there, Cassidy?" he asked.

It took a few seconds for the mouse's image to appear on the screen.

"Yes, I'm here," Cassidy replied. "I'm about to start the first dive . . ."

"Are you sure the jewel is underwater?" Klawitz asked, skeptical.

"Yes, I'm sure," Cassidy replied. "I am convinced the treasure will be found here, in the depths of Abū Qīr Bay. This is the exact spot where Cleopatra's palace sank into the water.

"I hope you're right," Klawitz replied, raising an eyebrow. "I've had quite enough of this game of find the treasure. It's time for the jewel to be in my paws at last!"

"I am confident that the secret underwater

expedition I organized will be a success!" Cassidy replied.

"How can you be so sure?" Klawitz prodded her.

CLEOPATRA'S SUBMERGED PALACE

In the 1990s, a team of archaeologists discovered a sunken island in the waters off Egypt's port of Alexandria. The island, Antirhodos, was home to Queen Cleopatra's palace. Scientists believe the island and palace sunk into the water around 300 AD after a terrible earthquake and tsunami struck Alexandria.

"The Sahara would have been an easy answer. Aurora was too clever, and her riddles are much harder than that. Her clue was pointing to Egypt, and even though the Sahara made sense, it was too **obvious**! I'm sure Cleopatra kept her beloved jewel close to her, and what place was closer than her own palace?"

"That makes sense," Klawitz agreed.

"Why don't you join me for the dive, sir?" Cassidy suggested. "I feel certain we will soon have our paws on the treasure. You won't want to miss it!"

"I'll think about it," Klawtiz replied, stroking his chin. "I'm not sure I have the time. I'm a very busy mouse. Now get back to work!"

Then he ended the call without saying good-bye.

"I have a choice to make. I can follow Cassidy or follow the Thea Sisters," Klawtiz mumbled to himself. "But first I want to check something."

He picked up a small **remote control** and pressed a button, activating a large screen on the wall behind him. He turned and carefully observed the scene, which was being filmed by one of his **high-tech** drones in Bolivia.

He saw the Thea Sisters and Irina Lenenko's brother chatting with a waitress inside what looked like a **restaurant**. The group was joking and laughing as if they were simply on a vacation.

"It doesn't look like those **nosy mice** are searching for Aurora Beatrix Lane's treasure

anymore," he said aloud. "They don't seem to be in too much of a hurry, at least. Maybe Cassidy is right: I should join her in Egypt. And if I'm wrong, I still have someone tailing those six busybodies in South America . . ."

His decision was made. Luke von Klawitz finally turned off the SCREENS in his lab and headed to the room where he kept everything he needed for sudden departures. In just a few minutes, he would be on his way to **Alexandria**!

DAWN IN THE DESERT

Early the next morning, the Thea Sisters and Sergei climbed out of their comfy beds in the darkness of the salt hotel.

"I still don't understand why we had to get up at this hour!" Violet protested between sleepy yawns.

"The Salar is huge!" Nicky reminded her friend. "We have to take advantage of every second today to look for Aurora's treasure!"

"Come on, let's get moving!" Pam squeaked enthusiastically as she loaded the trunk of the

I'm so sleepy!

SUV with supplies before she climbed into the driver's seat. The rest of the group climbed into the back of the SUV. As Pamela steered their vehicle out onto the salt flat, Sergei opened his laptop and looked at satellite images of the area.

"It would take at least three days to **EXPLORE** the entire desert," he explained. "Let's hope we are lucky enough to come across a clue right away!"

The sun began to rise slowly, illuminating the expanse of salt in a PINK light.

"Wow!" Violet exclaimed as she peered out the window. "This is one of the most spectacular landscapes I've ever seen! It feels like we're in a fairy tale."

"And it's all pink!" Colette added enthusiastically.

"It's so strange," Nicky remarked. "Even though I know its salt, I can't help but think it looks like a sheet of ICE!"

"I know what you mean," Sergei agreed.

"Can we get out for a second?" Colette asked. "It's so beautiful, I can't resist!"

"Yes, let's stop to stretch our legs and take a few photos," Violet said.

Ohhhh! Can we get out?

Pam stopped the car, and everyone climbed out eagerly.

"Isn't it amazing to think Aurora

admired this very same landscape so many years ago?" Violet said quietly.

"It's hard to believe!" Paulina replied. "I'm sure she saw many incredible things in her career as an **archaeologist**. I wonder if her heart was still full of **wonder** when she saw these salt flats."

"I'm sure it was," Sergei said, smiling.

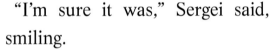

"I think it's time for us to get back to our **MISSION**," Nicky reminded the others. "We still have to find Cleopatra's emerald."

The group got back in the car, ready to explore the Salar. For the next two hours, Pam drove slowly across the immense salt flat. Meanwhile, the others observed the **landscape** carefully, looking for clues.

Then, without warning, Pam stopped the car.

"Pam, what's the matter?" Paulina asked.

"My stomach doesn't feel so great," Pam explained. "We skipped **breakfast**!"

"Okay, let's take a twenty-minute break to eat," Nicky said. "Then we'll get back to exploring!"

Pam opened her backpack and pulled out provisions for a late breakfast, including bread, dulce de leche,* and a **cake**.

As everyone ate, Paulina snapped **photos** of the landscape.

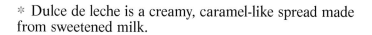

* Dulce de leche is a creamy, caramel-like spread made from sweetened milk.

"Hey, look at how this photo came out," Paulina exclaimed, chuckling. She showed her friends the image on her phone. "It's **INCREDIBLE**!"

In the picture, Colette was standing in the desert, eating a sandwich. But thanks to the vast expanse of desert in front and behind her, it looked as though she was standing on top of a gigantic jar of dulce de leche!

"Wow!" Pam exclaimed, astounded. "How did you do that?"

"The image is an optical illusion," Sergei said, laughing.

"Can we try another pose?" Colette asked, curiously.

For the next few minutes, the friends forgot all about their mission as they experimented with different fun poses against the unusual desert backdrop.

Nicky sleeping on a mug!

Walking across a braid!

Balancing on a water bottle!

"**How fun!**" Paulina and Sergei said as they flipped through the images on Paulina's phone.

Violet glanced at her watch and gave a **start**.

"We can't linger any longer," she said. "Let's get back to our search!"

READING BETWEEN THE LINES

The group climbed back into the SUV and continued their journey across the desert. They drove on and on through the **mesmerizing** landscape.

"I'm starting to get a huge headache from staring out the window at all of this salt," Colette said.

"I know," Nicky agreed. "We've been driving for **hours**, but we haven't found any clues. It's very frustrating."

"Maybe we should take another look at Aurora's **DiaRY**!" Violet exclaimed suddenly. "She wrote everything down. She must have written something about her travels in Bolivia, too . . ."

September 16

Of all the ancient civilizations, the pre-Columbian architectural complex of Pumapunku (which means "the door of the puma" in the ancient language of Aymara) is one of the most mysterious. This Bolivian archaeological site includes the remains of a temple built between 500 and 1000 AD.

I glued a photograph here of a structure called The Gate of the Sun.

I am astounded by the accomplishments of these ancient mice, so many years ago. It is such a joy to explore these artifacts of the past. Whenever I uncover a lost treasure or put together the clues to answer a puzzling question about how these incredible mice lived, I feel as though I am flying through the air like a golden eagle!

And today I am here on a special mission. I have promised myself I will do all I can to combat greed and ignorance. It isn't easy, but I know I can do it. I must reach the island in the desert. Once there I will bury the queen's treasure in a fish's stomach covered in very fine thorns . . .

"I really don't understand what she's writing about," Pam said, shaking her head. "She talks about pumas, golden eagles, and fish. It seems like an essay on **ANIMALS** rather than archaeology!"

"But she mentions the queen's treasure!" Nicky exclaimed. "Surely that's a reference to Cleopatra's jewel, right?"

"I think so," Colette said. "But what **exactly** is she trying to tell us?"

"Reach an island in the desert . . ." Paulina reflected. "How can there be an island in the desert? It seems like a poem that doesn't make any sense."

"And what does she mean that she will bury the queen's treasure in a fish's stomach covered in very fine thorns?" Violet wondered aloud. "We're in the desert — there are no fish here!"

Suddenly, Sergei smacked his forehead with his paw.

"Of course!" he squeaked. "Pam, turn left and let's drive!"

"But where are we going?" Paulina asked.

"You'll see," Sergei replied, his eyes sparkling. "I think I know where Aurora hid the treasure!"

THE FISH'S STOMACH

Pam followed Sergei's instructions and turned the SUV to the left.

"Wherever we're going, I hope it isn't **FAR**," she said. "I feel like I've been driving for an entire month!"

"You have been driving for a while," Sergei agreed. "Do you want to take a **BREAK**?"

"I have to admit that I'm exhausted," Pam said, stopping the car. "Thanks for taking over, Sergei!"

"I hope you're right," Colette said as Sergei climbed into the driver's seat.

"Don't worry," Sergei replied, smiling. "I'm feeling really good about this!"

After driving for another half hour, they arrived at a **ROCKY** piece of land that stood in the middle of the white expanse of desert.

"It looks like an island in a sea of salt," Violet said as she and her friends got out of the car.

Here we are!

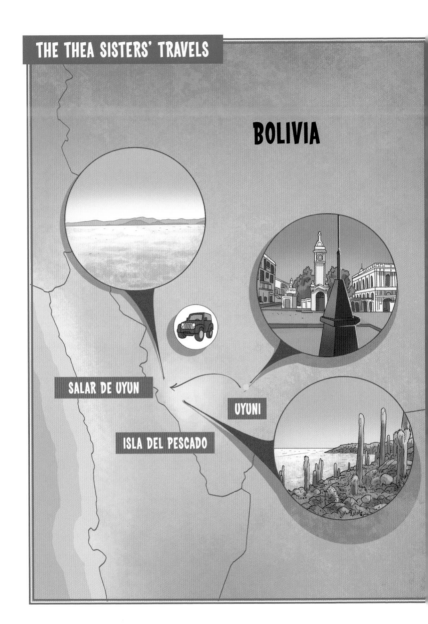

THE THEA SISTERS' TRAVELS

BOLIVIA

SALAR DE UYUN

UYUNI

ISLA DEL PESCADO

"Here it is!" Sergei said proudly. "The **Isla del Pescado**. It's a rocky hill that emerges from the ground like an island. Remember? Adriana told us about it at dinner last night!"

"Yes!" Paulina exclaimed. "And *pescado* means 'fish' in Spanish! So this must be the fish from Aurora's diary!"

"Yes, I think so," Sergei agreed. "I had seen this island on the map, and when I heard the word *fish*, something clicked."

"Are those **cacti** up there?" Nicky asked, shading her eyes with her paw to see.

"Ah, the very fine thorns Aurora describes . . ." Violet said, smiling. "Amazing detective work, Sergei!"

The friends set about exploring the island.

"It seemed smaller on the map," Sergei said as they walked along the island trails, which were lined with **TALL**, skinny cacti.

"Every time we think we're getting close to solving Aurora's puzzle, things get more complicated," Paulina said.

"Why don't I go for a little JOG?" Nicky offered. "I'll be able to cover more ground."

She leaped forward to start her run, but in doing so, she **bumped** into Violet, who dropped Aurora's diary.

"Sorry, Vi!" Nicky exclaimed as she bent down to pick up the book. Then she stopped in her tracks. "Wait a minute . . ."

"**What is it?**" Pam asked as she peered over Nicky's shoulder at the diary.

Look!

The book was open to the page that mentioned Aurora's trip to Bolivia.

Nicky pointed to the drawing of the fish at the bottom of the page.

"This isn't a simple sketch!" she exclaimed. "These scales are actually tiny **numbers**!"

"Let me see," Paulina said, taking the diary in her paws. "**YOU'RE RIGHT!** They're coordinates. Maybe these are the exact coordinates of the point where she hid the treasure!"

"Hello," came a sudden voice behind them.

LOST AND FOUND!

Sergei and the Thea Sisters were astounded to see their missing Egyptian friend, Omar, suddenly appear.

"Omar!" Colette exclaimed in surprise as she rushed to hug him. "We didn't know what had happened to you back in Egypt. Why didn't you respond to our **message**?"

"We were so worried," Paulina added. "But we didn't know how to reach you."

Nicky frowned.

"And what are you doing here now?" she asked.

Omar seemed embarrassed.

"I ran off when those henchmice arrived," he admitted. "And then I managed to lose

Omar!

my cell phone. But I knew that you all would be worried. So as soon as I figured out Aurora's riddle was referring to a desert of salt and not sand, I came to Bolivia. I was sure I would find you all here, in the Salar de Uyuni!"

"And how did you figure out **exactly** where we were?" Sergei asked, astounded by Omar's tale.

"By chance!" Omar replied, smiling. "I was exploring the desert when in the distance I saw six mice getting out of an SUV to climb this island. I recognized all of you and I came right over!"

"**Amazing!**" Pam said. "You arrived at just the right moment: We are close to finding the treasure!"

"Really?" Omar asked immediately. "Where is it?"

"Follow us and you'll see," Paulina replied. She had just tapped the coordinates from Aurora's diary into the GPS navigator on her **cell phone**.

It was a long walk, but the time passed quickly. The Thea Sisters were excited to have found their friend and to be so close to the queen's jewel.

"Another five hundred feet and we'll be there!" Paulina said. "The treasure is . . . right down there!"

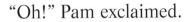

"Oh!" Pam exclaimed.

Paulina was pointing to an area that was down a steep embankment that was covered in **SHARP** rocks and cacti.

"How do we get down there?" Colette asked, disappointed at the setback.

"Carefully," Nicky replied. "Let's go down one at a time. I'll go first."

Nicky made her way down **carefully**, followed by the others. Soon the group found themselves at the entrance to a **CAVE** in the rock.

Some loose boulders

Be careful!

blocked the entrance, but Sergei, Omar, and the Thea Sisters worked together to move the rocks aside.

"Here we go," Nicky said as she stepped into the **DARK** cave.

Pam followed her, illuminating the way with a FLASHLIGHT she had pulled out of her backpack. In the corner of the cave, the beam of light landed on what looked like a sparkling treasure chest

"The queen's jewel," Colette gasped.

DEAD IN THE WATER

A thin beam of light **LIT UP** the dark water in front of Luke von Klawitz and his assistant Cassidy. Suddenly, the proud profile of a stone lion **appeared**. Klawitz turned and swam away from the lion. As cool as the statue looked, it wasn't the treasure he was looking for. Klawitz approached another sunken statue half-buried in the sand. This one was a **GRANITE** face resting at the bottom of the sea.

Even though the mice couldn't squeak underwater, Cassidy knew her boss was angry. The **dives** had gone on for a while, but they hadn't found a trace of Cleopatra's **EMERALD**.

Klawitz was fed up. He gestured to Cassidy that he wanted to return to the surface. She quickly followed.

"Enough," he said gruffly as he removed his scuba mask. "It's clear that we aren't going to find the treasure underwater. I don't know why I let you convince me this was where I would finally find the queen's jewel."

"I think we just need to search a little longer," Cassidy protested. "The gem has been down here for centuries — the sand probably covered it, or maybe the tides moved it."

"That's enough!" Klawitz thundered. "We're done diving for sunken treasure. I'm leaving Egypt in **THREE HOURS**. You have exactly that much time to figure out where the treasure really is."

Cassidy's fur PALED.

"Th-three hours?" she stuttered. "I guess it's possible the gem is somewhere in the Sahara —"

"Max and Stan already tried the desert," Klawitz replied. "And they were wrong. Any other ideas?"

"Maybe we should start over?" she ventured. "We could figure out where the Thea Sisters are and follow them like we did the last time."

Th-three hours?!

"Those busymice are on vacation in South America," he scoffed. "I don't know what they're up to, but it has nothing to do with Aurora Beatrix Lane's treasure."

Suddenly, Klawitz's watch vibrated.

"Now if you'll excuse me, I have **REAL** work to do," he told Cassidy before he stormed off.

Klawitz headed back to the large **BLACK** car that was parked near the beach where he and Cassidy had been diving. He climbed

Hmmm . . .

into the back seat and *immediately* turned on the built-in computer monitor. After a second, a message appeared:

The jewel is in sight.

Klawitz rubbed his paws together greedily.

"My **SECRET** weapon worked after all," he muttered. "Excellent!"

"Take me to my jet immediately," he ordered his driver. "Call ahead to let the pilot know to prepare for departure. I'm leaving for Bolivia **right away**!"

A BEAUTIFUL DISCOVERY

Colette picked up the small chest to take a closer look.

"It's dark in here," Nicky said. "Let's go into the light and open it there."

Everyone hurried out of the cave, where the bright sunlight BLINDED them for a moment.

"Go ahead, Coco, open it!" Pam said as soon as her eyes had adjusted to the daylight.

Colette took a deep breath and slowly opened the box.

"It's . . . an old piece of cloth," Colette announced.

Omar stepped up to the box and grabbed the piece of fabric. He quickly unwrapped it, revealing a **dazzling** green stone.

"I did . . . I mean, we did it!" he exclaimed

Wrapped in the fabric was the **stone**. It was a shade of green that none of the mice had ever seen in **nature**.

"We found the queen's jewel!" Colette said in awe

It's a piece of fabric . . .

as she took the gem from Omar and gently put it back into the box. "It's so beautiful!"

"Now it can be displayed for the whole world to see," Violet said happily. "It's a treasure for EVERYONE!"

"Aurora would be so pleased," Nicky added. "We've kept the gem away from the greedy Klawitz family, and now it can be donated to a museum!"

"Great work!" Paulina agreed.

"Yes, yes," Omar said seriously. "It's a very precious treasure, and we must be careful with it. Let's close the box right away!"

Pam was taken aback by Omar's sudden **intensity**.

"Relax, Omar," she said. "The gem is safe. You're taking this mission almost more seriously than we are!"

"Well, it's an **important** mission," Omar replied. "And I feel invested in the outcome. Since I have to return to Egypt myself, I would be honored to bring the emerald to Cairo to entrust it to the Egyptian Museum. What do you say?"

"Well . . ." Colette began, but before she could say another word, an unusual sound interrupted her.

GRRRRRRRRR . . .

"What's that?" Nicky asked.

"I think it's that bird!" Pamela replied, pointing at a large feathered creature with a long neck that was running straight at them.

"Oh, oh!" Omar exclaimed as he found himself right in the bird's path.

Everyone backed away quickly, but the bird suddenly *ACCELERATED* and pumped up its plumage, heading straight at Omar.

"**HELP!**" Omar cried, and he took off running in the opposite direction, the bird chasing close behind him.

"I'll handle it," Paulina said confidently.

She approached the bird calmly and slowly, and carefully patted its head. Then she firmly but gently led the bird away from the group. A minute or so later, the bird seemed to have calmed down and it walked away quietly.

Omar breathed a sigh of relief. "Thank you," he said. "What was that thing?"

"It was a rhea!" Paulina explained.

"A . . . what?" Pam asked.

"A **RHEA**," Paulina repeated. "They're similar to emus. I've seen them from time to time in Peru. Luckily, this one wasn't too **BiG**!"

"I wonder what it had against me," Omar muttered, shaking his head.

"Sometimes rheas can **attack** for no reason," Paulina explained. "I don't think it really had anything against you."

In the commotion, something had fallen out of Omar's pocket. Colette noticed it and bent down to pick up a small blue notebook.

"Colette!" Nicky called out. "Let's go! We're heading to the SUV!"

"I'm coming!" Colette replied, quickly slipping the book into her pocket as she hurried to the car.

What's this?

THE BEST PLAN

Their mission accomplished, the Thea Sisters and Sergei were **excited** to return to Uyuni for their flight back to Moscow.

Omar had parked his SUV not far from theirs, and they all walked toward the cars together.

"As I said, if you give me the emerald, I can safely bring it to the Egyptian Museum in Cairo," Omar told them as he approached his car.

I don't think so ...

"Actually, I don't think that's the best plan," Violet replied.

"Me neither," Nicky added. "We followed the clues from **Russia** to **Egypt** and now to

BOLiVia. We need time to figure out our next steps!"

"I agree," Pam said. "We need to be sure the emerald doesn't fall into the wrong paws. We started this mission, and we should finish it."

"I agree," Sergei said. "The Thea Sisters should be the ones —"

"Enough!" Omar said, cutting off Sergei and **STARTLiNG** the others. "You all know me well enough by now. You can **trust** me!"

"It's not that we don't trust you," Sergei said immediately. "But you would be traveling alone, while there are **SIX** of us. We have a much better chance of protecting the jewel if we should run into Luke von Klawitz or some other **unscrupulous** mouse or mice."

"I said I could do it!" Omar said, frustrated. "Now give me the EMERALD."

He took a step closer to Colette, who was holding the box.

"Omar, what's wrong with you?" Pam urged him. "**Calm down!**"

But Omar ignored Pam and instead took

I want the emerald!

What are you doing?

another step toward Colette. Nicky stepped between them.

"What are you doing?" she asked Omar.

Without squeaking another word, Omar pushed Nicky aside and grabbed the box.

"If you won't trust me with it, I'll just have to **TAKE IT**!" he said, his friendly look changing to an ugly sneer.

But . . . what?!

"Don't you **do-gooders** understand? I don't care about any of you or about Aurora. This treasure is going to make me rich!"

With that, he leaped toward his car, jumped in, and took off at top speed, his tires **spinning**. The Thea Sisters and Sergei were left standing there in shock, covered in tiny flecks of **salt**.

"Oh no!" Pam exclaimed as Omar's car grew smaller and smaller.

"I can't believe it!" Sergei yelled, astonished. "Omar didn't want to help us. He only wanted to get his paws on the jewel!"

"We trusted him," Violet said, tears in her eyes. "I can't believe we didn't realize he had the **worst** intentions!"

"Let's go!" Nicky said decisively as she sprinted toward the SUV. "There's no time to lose. We have to **FOLLOW HIM**!"

Let's go!

YOU ARE A
GENIUS, COCO!

But Colette grabbed Nicky by the wrist.

"No, stop!" she protested. "Let him go."

"What?!" Paulina exclaimed. "But we need to follow Omar! He took the emerald!"

"No, he didn't," Colette replied, smiling mysteriously. "Don't worry. Everything is okay."

"What are you squeaking about, Coco?!" Pam asked, scratching her head.

Colette reached into the pocket inside her pink jacket and pulled something out. It was a sparkling green stone.

"I d-don't believe it," Violet stuttered, amazed. "But that's . . ."

"Cleopatra's EMERALD," Colette confirmed.

I have it!

"What did I tell you? There was nothing to worry about!"

The Thea Sisters and Sergei gathered around Colette, hugging her and peppering her with questions:

"But how did you do it?"

"When did you hide it?"

"How did you know about Omar?"

"When the rhea attacked Omar, something fell out of his pocket," Colette explained. "I picked it up and was about to give it back to him when I noticed this."

She pulled another item from her pocket and showed it to her friends. It was Omar's blue **notebook**.

"What?!" Paulina exclaimed in surprise.

292

"That's the symbol for Luke von Klawitz's company!"

"What?!" Nicky gasped. "So Omar has been working for Klawitz this entire time? I can't believe it!"

"I know," Colette said. "I didn't believe it at first, either. But then the pieces fell into place. Omar's disappearance in Egypt was so strange, and then he just reappeared in Bolivia without warning. I realized Omar was after the emerald, and I slipped his notebook into my pocket without letting him see."

"You are a genius!" Pam exclaimed as she gave her friend a tight hug.

"Now we really need to go," Sergei reminded them. "We have to get the jewel somewhere safe as soon as possible!"

Everyone climbed into the SUV, and Pam drove toward Uyuni. Once they arrived, the Thea Sisters spoke with the authorities there and came up with a plan to get the EMERALD into the right paws.

Their mission complete, the group headed to the airport for their flight to **Moscow**. Their incredible adventure had finally reached its end.

"Omar is carrying around an empty box, right?" Violet asked Colette as they waited in the departures area.

"Not exactly," Colette replied, chuckling. "Let's just say there's a little SURPRISE for him inside . . ."

THE LAST TRICK

After many hours of driving, Omar finally arrived in La Paz, Bolivia. When he spoke to Klawitz about the treasure, his boss had agreed to meet him in Bolivia immediately.

"Good evening," Omar said to the doorman of the luxurious hotel where he was meeting his boss. "I'm Omar, and I'm here to see Luke von Klawitz."

The doorman nodded and smiled. "The gentlemice are waiting for you by the pool. It's the last door on the left."

Clutching the old, dented tin box, Omar STRODE down the hallway.

"Welcome," Klawitz said without turning around. "We have been waiting for you."

"It's an HONOR to see you, sir," Omar began.

"Enough small talk," Klawitz said immediately. "Did you bring it?"

"Yes, here it is," Omar replied, giving his boss the box. "Those mice from Mouseford and their Russian friend tried to stop me, but I was determined. And to show my loyalty to you, I decided not to open the box. The honor is all yours, sir."

"Excellent," Klawitz muttered as he rubbed his paws together eagerly.

Omar closed his eyes, and waited for the compliments he would get once his boss saw the glittering emerald. He would finally be repaid for all the time and effort he had put into befriending the Thea Sisters and following them from one continent to the next.

But suddenly an unexpected sound filled

the room. It was Luke von Klawitz, and he was squeaking at the top of his lungs. Stan and Max were so **SURPRISED** that they almost fell in the pool.

"WHAT IS THIS?!"

Luke von Klawitz showed Omar the contents of the box.

"No!" Omar gasped. "It can't be. Where

is the **EMERALD**?! I d-don't understand."

Klawitz held a pink tube of strawberry-flavored **lip gloss**.

"You're fired," Klawitz told Omar. "I don't want to see your snout ever again."

Omar DASHED out of the room.

Grrrr!

A second later, Klawitz tossed the box away in a rage. It landed in the pool with a splash. And that was the end of Luke von Klawitz's search for Cleopatra's precious emerald, one the world's seven great treasures.

AN UNEXPECTED SURPRISE

The Thea Sisters and Sergei landed in Moscow and scampered off the plane, excited to see Sergei's sister, **Irina**. But they couldn't find her anywhere!

Oh ...

Sergei turned on his phone and his shoulders sagged with **disappointment**.

"My sister sent me a message," he explained. "She said she doesn't have time to come get us and that we should take a cab straight home."

"It's okay," Pam said sympathetically. "We crossed half the world to find Cleopatra's

302

emerald. We'll be able to get from the airport to your home in **no time**!"

Sergei smiled. "You're right. Let's go!"

Less than an hour later, they arrived at Sergei's home. Sergei looked up at the window.

"How strange," he said. "I don't see any LIGHTS in the window. I wonder if Irina is home."

"Maybe she had to work late at the lab," Paulina guessed.

"I'm sure she'll be home SOON!" Pam said.

Sergei put the key in the lock and turned. "I can't wait —"

"SURPRISE!"

The light suddenly came on and Sergei and the Thea Sisters were greeted by a smiling Irina and a group of her friends.

"I wanted to thank you for SAVING ME and for finding our great-aunt's treasure!" Irina said as she threw her arms around her brother. "I've never been so proud of you!"

"Thank you," Sergei replied, his cheeks turning red. "But it's really all thanks for the Thea Sisters. I couldn't have done it without their help!"

Thanks!

"We were a great TEAM," Paulina agreed.

"Let me introduce you to some of my friends," Irina said.

The apartment was decorated for the party, with tables full of drinks and tasty food. Cheerful music played in the background, and the Thea Sisters enjoyed meeting everyone.

Paulina was standing a bit apart from everyone.

"Are you okay?" Sergei asked as he approached her.

"Yes," she replied. "I'm just sorry this trip is over! It was an incredible experience, and I'm so glad we met and had the chance to become good friends!"

"I was thinking the same thing," Sergei replied. "I would love to come visit you all at Mouseford one day!"

"That would be FANTASTIC," Paulina replied, smiling.

"And now let's dance!" Sergei said.

"Great idea!" Paulina replied. Then she, Sergei, Pam, Nicky, Colette, and Violet spent the rest of the night dancing and enjoying their last unforgettable night in Moscow.

A DIARY FOR FIVE

The following morning, Sergei took the Thea Sisters to the airport.

"Have a good trip," he told them. *See you soon!* "And please be careful of fake tour guides and greedy TREASURE HUNTERS!"

"You can say that again!" Pam said with a laugh.

After one last hug, the THEA SISTERS boarded the plane that would bring them back to Whale Island.

"Vi, sit near me!" Nicky said. "You have Aurora's diary, right? I want to read some more. I'm not quite ready for our **ADVENTURE** to end!"

Violet pulled out the diary. She was about to open it to read aloud when Colette interrupted.

"I just had the most **terrific** idea," Colette said eagerly. "What do you think about us keeping a **diary** about our adventures, just like Aurora Beatrix Lane? We could write about the discoveries we've made thanks to her!"

"That would be **FANTASTIC**!" Paulina exclaimed. "Our adventurous travels in search of the seven treasures should absolutely be recorded!"

"We'd be following in Aurora's **pawsteps**," Violet added. "We can leave a written testimony, just as she did with her diaries!"

"I have something that will help us," Colette added cheerfully. She reached into

The five of us . . . dressed like Aurora!

her purse and pulled out a **PiNK** notebook.

"I would have chosen another **color** myself, but since it was your idea, I think that's fair," Nicky teased her friend.

"Where should we begin?" Pam asked.

"At the beginning!" Violet replied, and she began to write . . .

It all began in
Scotland . . .

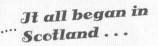

Where we found a
tapestry . . .

. . . with Aurora's
treasure map!

The treasure
belonged to
Mumtaz Mahal!

To find the
treasure, we
first went to
Mexico . . .

And in the
end, we
found the
alabaster
garden!

Our vacation in Moscow!

We found clues to a new treasure, the queen's jewel!

The gem was an emerald that had been Cleopatra's.

We visited the Sahara looking for the jewel . . .

But the quest led us to Bolivia!

Violet closed the notebook on their adventures and put it in her bag, along with *Aurora's* diary.

"That's all for now," she said.

"Yes, for now," Colette agreed, smiling. "But something tells me that our **ADVENTURES** as treasure hunters aren't finished yet!"